THE LIBERATED

STAR TREK
DEEP SPACE NINE®

REBELS

BOOK THREE OF THREE

THE LIBERATED

Dafydd ab Hugh

POCKET BOOKS
New York   London   Toronto   Sydney   Tokyo   Singapore

This book is a work of fiction. Names, characters, places and incidents are products of the author's imagination or are used fictitiously. Any resemblance to actual events or locales or persons, living or dead, is entirely coincidental.

An *Original* Publication of POCKET BOOKS

POCKET BOOKS, a division of Simon & Schuster Inc.
1230 Avenue of the Americas, New York, NY 10020

STAR TREK is a Registered Trademark of Paramount Pictures.

A VIACOM COMPANY

This book is published by Pocket Books, a division of Simon & Schuster Inc., under exclusive license from Paramount Pictures.

ISBN: 0-671-01142-1

First Pocket Books printing March 1999

10 9 8 7 6 5 4 3 2 1

POCKET and colophon are registered trademarks of Simon & Schuster Inc.

Printed in the U.S.A.

THE LIBERATED

CHAPTER
1

MAJOR KIRA NERYS stood rigid, forcing her body not to tremble in suppressed anger and humiliation. It was all the Bajoran freedom fighter could do not to leap across the brief gap and throttle the black-clad, black-helmeted alien "dean" who now commanded *Deep Space Nine* . . . or *Emissary's Sanctuary*, as Kai Winn had renamed it—the same Kai Winn who had just surrendered the station to the "Liberated," as the invaders had called themselves.

The Liberated said little but the necessary. But that was a welcome change from the more loathsome, loquatious representatives of the Dominion, the Vorta—and from the harsh Jem'Hadar, who would already have slapped a restraining field on Kira, the Kai, and the other Bajorans. These unknowns were gentle, at least, now that they'd won the station. *Have to change the name to Hot Potato,* thought Kira with a curled lip, *the way we're passing it around from hand to hand.* Living among humans had taught her many old Earth expressions.

"Courage, child," said the Kai in a monumentally condescending attempt at raising Kira's spirits. "The Prophets send tribulations to test us."

"Did you say that during the Occupation, too?" The words were out before Kira could swallow them, but she was secretly glad she'd said it: too many people, herself included, tiptoed around the blind, stubborn Kai Winn as if she were a glacier, unturnable and irresistible.

"Yes, child, I did." Winn turned to stare at Kira's face, bringing a flush of self-consciousness to the major's cheek. Kira kept her eyes on the invader dean, who was quietly ordering his troops into quite an effective occupation of all three Promenade levels. "And at last, we passed that test," said the Kai.

Kira clenched her teeth so hard, she felt one of them crack. There was nothing she could do but obey the dean's last order to stand still and not move: Kai Winn, Kira's commanding officer and governor of the station, had surrendered to the Liberated, and the Bajoran frigates had backed far enough away not to be a factor. *Not that they could have done anything but die gallantly,* she thought, tasting another lump of bile; *we were outgunned, out fought, and out thought.* Already, the ghosts of three hundred Bajoran souls haunted Kira Nerys—the number lost in the first naval wave sent by Bajor to reinforce the *Emissary's Sanctuary* and its governor, the Kai.

Kira snuck a glance to her right. The Kai wore a sweet smile, the vapid mask of "serenity" that Kira had learned hid a capable and determined middle-aged woman, a true leader of her beleaguered people. Kira fought the illusion that Kai Winn projected. The major struggled to remember that Winn could be as bloodthirsty and dangerous as any Resistance fighter, no matter how much or little she might have done during the Resistance. *We fought in different ways,* Kira caught herself thinking; *now my way is futile . . . could the Kai Winn route still be viable?*

The futility of fighting had been demonstrated to Kira a few scant minutes after she and the Kai met the alien dean on the Promenade three hours ago. Then, Kira had been her angry self, coldly confronting the dean and demanding, demanding . . . what? Everything: that the prisoners be treated gently, that the station integrity be respected, that the Liberated apologize, beg forgiveness, and *get off Deep Space Nine!* But Kai Winn passed on an opportunity to back up her executive officer, offering only that the name of the station was *Emissary's Sanctuary* now.

Furious, Kira turned on her Kai. "That's it? That's *all* you can say?"

Winn smiled gently through the tirade, irritating Kira even further. "Child, the Way of the Prophets is not the child's blind resistance to authority. I'm sure our new masters will be kind to the Bajorans, who freely offer to share the Orb, the far-seeing anomaly." Kai Winn turned to the dean. "Won't you?"

"Bajorans will not be harmed," said the universal-translator implant in Kira's head, the clicking and buzzing of the alien's actual speech an annoying background noise.

"And what about those who aren't Bajorans?" asked Kira, beginning to tremble as she held back a wall of rage. "Jake Sisko, and Nog, and—and Garak." *Did I really just say that, fretting for the safety of that butcher?* "And what about our freedom? Is that just another casualty of war?"

She was shouting at the dean, but her fury was directed more at Kai Winn for her betrayal. Dropping her hands to her side, Kira's thumb brushed the combat knife she still carried. She had of course surrendered her phaser rifle and hand phaser, but she had conveniently forgotten about the largely ceremonial *"kolba's* tooth" commando knife, which she had worn all through the Resistance. Then, though used only once to kill, it had come in handy a thousand times to open a food pack or cut a fishing line.

Without thinking, her hand curled around the wooden haft. She slid it from the sheathe, silent as the grave, and concealed it up behind her forearm. Kira glanced at the Kai . . . but she could never turn her wrath on one annointed by the Prophets, no matter what the betrayal. *Kai Winn will never get a knife in the back from me, whatever the provocation.*

At that moment the alien dean turned *his* back to order a complete search of all buildings on the Promenade. Kira had a single chance and took it. She leapt the short distance, thrusting directly forward with the blade in a brutal and efficient lunge.

Evidently the Liberated boasted significantly quicker reaction time than Bajorans. The dean barely glanced back over his shoulder as he hooked his foot up and slightly deflected Kira's lunge, which missed wide. Giving her a gentle push in the direction she was already moving, he flung Kira to the ground with disturbing ease. Then he picked up his conversation where he'd left off. Meanwhile, three other aliens dogpiled on Kira's back, wrenching the knife from her grasp and nearly breaking her wrist in the bargain.

The black-clad invaders were anonymous, their heads in tight-fitting, opaque helmets, or so Kira originally thought. Close up, she saw there were no helmets. Their faces were featureless cyphers, and she felt her stomach turn despite long exposure to disgusting aliens. *Sensory organs buried inside,* she realized; *built to withstand terrible punishment.* Feeling the hardness of the bodies pinning her, she understood with revulsion that they wore no armor, as she first imagined: their outer skin was an insect-like carapace covered only with a layer of metallic clothing. They needed no suits or helmets, not even to cross the abyss of space between their ships and the station, nothing but what looked like some kind of foil, to protect them against the background cosmic radiation. Perfect killing machines.

And they let her up. Her captors helped Kira to her feet and didn't even bother binding her hands. They even gave her back her knife. Burning with humiliation, Kira shuffled back to stand alongside her Kai . . . who throughout her attempt had never stopped negotiating diplomatically with the dean. *I'm not the slightest threat to them,* Major Kira realized. *I'm a child with a toy sword.*

Hours later she still felt the dull ache of useless-
ness, the same claustrophobic feeling of horror that
had driven her to join the Resistance at such a young
age. Today, however, there was no outlet. Kira's
shoulders slumped, and she could barely work up
the energy for verbal defiance.

One certainty echoed through her head: despite
the Kai's seeming surrender, she knew that Winn
had no intention of giving up either control of the
station or hegemony in Bajor, that she would never
voluntarily turn over so much power.

Kai Winn must have a plan, some plan, some
amazing, unexpected plan that would cast out the
tide and reclaim the dry land! If Major Kira could
only control her temper and work with Kai Winn,
together they still had a chance—many chances—to
unspill the water jug.

. . . Or at least, any other thought was intolerable
to the major. Bajorans, and most especially Kira
Nerys, could not live without hope. And the most
burning desire in Kira's stomach, she admitted to
herself shamefully, was to live through the ordeal—
to survive.

Light-years away, on a strange and different world,
Security Chief Odo sat rigidly on an overturned
barrel, puzzling over the sheaf of documents Tivva-
ma, daughter of hereditary Mayor Asta-ha, had just
shoved into his hands.

Odo pored over the pages she had scrawled on in
her childish hand. At first, he humored her: he began
a suitable period of study, to be followed by a pat on
the head and some encouraging words.

But as he read section after section, Odo became so enthralled he forgot even to simulate breath. What Tivva-ma had pushed into his indulgent hands was less a manifesto, as she had claimed, than a *fully developed constitution* for a complex trade republic; it included a declaration of rights and duties that balanced so nicely, Odo thought the United Federation of Planets might want to take a look.

"Tivva-ma, where did you say you got this?"

The girl put her hands over her eyes, shyly refusing to answer.

"Did your mother work it out?" She grunted, meaning No. "Owena-da? One of the away—one of us officers?"

"Uh-uh." Abruptly, the waif threw her arms wide, exposing a huge grin set against her pale blue hair and alabaster skin. "I did!"

Odo slowly lowered the pages into his lap, restraining the pulse of excitement that whirled round his mind, which was his whole body. *Easy, easy. Maybe she didn't understand the question. Maybe she's lying or mistaken.* Choosing his most imperious schoolmaster tone, he began to question Tivva-ma about specifics and particulars. But at every query, he was satisfied: the tot knew the proposal backward and forward, at least. And in her squeaky, little-girl voice, she defended the provisions from all attack, whether the tricameral judicial legislature, the ceremonial and functional presidents, the selection and evaluation criteria for government officials, or the minimalist nature of state authority. After a quarter hour of discussion Odo was reeling from her observations, calling into question as they did everything he had ever believed anent the value of law in guiding good behavior.

Odo rose, holding the pages carefully. He wanted to scan them into a computer and compare them to the constitutions of thousands of societies in the Federation memory banks . . . but a more important task loomed. "Child, what you have created is brilliant. You are a shining star. But we cannot set up a government until we have a society at least—a community!"

Tivva-ma gasped; her eyes showed she had been stunned by Odo's critique. *"That's* what I forgot! I *knew* I forgot something, but I couldn't remember what it was." The girl turned and sped like a lightning discharge back toward the temporary camp. She paused, just before the scattered trees that hid the shelters. "I'll be right back! Wait. . . ." Then she grinned sheepishly. "Actually, it might take a couple a days." She dashed away; if Odo had blinked, he would have missed her exit.

Suddenly freed from the darkness of techno-utopia, the Natives, as Commander Dax called them, had lit up as though suddenly electrified. They had been living their lives unchallenged, with nothing to tax the brain beyond a few peripatetic raids of one village by another, and the simple act of destroying the hemisphere's power grid had energized them like the spark of life. The socially infantile Natives flickered suddenly at the threshhold of intellectual puberty.

How far will they go? wondered the constable, looking nervously back over his shoulder at the away team's own camp. *How soon will the Tiffnaki surpass us? And what will they do then, when we're no longer useful to the them?* He snorted, taking refuge in sensible cynicism. They were still the same Natives: Mayor-General Asta-ha had once again changed the name of her villagers, the third time in the ten days since Captain Sisko, Odo, and the rest of the away team had blown the power generators: from Tiffnaki to Tivvnaffi to Vanaffi, and now to Vanimastavvi. So what if their IQs were already cruising past 200 on their way up? Their personalities had hardly changed—and that was a better measure of *who one was* than raw brain power. Or so the constable and the rest of the away team had told themselves at every opportunity.

He heard a terrible, hacking cough from Chief O'Brien. Odo felt a twinge of guilt that he alone of all the team members didn't experience the asthmatic agony produced by microscopic, poisonous algae in the atmosphere. Captain Sisko had concocted a slapdash antitoxin from his own emergency Medi-Kit, but it couldn't compensate for the algae anywhere near as well as Dr. Bashir's original had. *We must return to the Defiant,* thought Odo. But the *Defiant* had disappeared from orbit and was not communicating.

The constable heard a wild patter and someone screaming semicoherently. He leapt to his feet, already annoyed even before he recognized the owner of the bare feet pounding in the latinum-laced mud toward the constable. But he was struck dumb at the sight of mad Quark, naked save for a large, palm-like frond wrapped around his midsection, dashing like a frog monster toward Odo's "courthouse stump." The Ferengi's eyes were wide and wild, his skin a livid pink-tinged orange under the ruddy sun.

"Do something—do *something!* You—you—just *do something,* by the Final Accountant! Or I'll . . ." The Ferengi heaved and panted, gripping his frond, simultaneously enraged and humiliated.

"Oh dear, Quark. Mind snapped at last?" Odo tsk-tsked and turned back to Tivva-ma's astonishing constitution.

"I've been robbed! By force!" Quark mumbled something under his breath.

"What was that last part?" asked Odo, half-sure he knew what the Ferengi had said but wanting the pleasure of hearing it aloud.

Quark closed his eyes, took a deep breath, facing up to the latest outrage against his Ferengi sensibilities. "I said, I've been robbed by force—of fraud."

"Force of fraud? Is that what you call it?" Odo smirked, a talent he had perfected through long years of dealing with the Ferengi bartender. "In other words, your little Native friends, whom you've been swindling out of everything they owned before you came here—oh, I have notes!—and I'm going to file quite an interesting report when we get back to the station . . . your friends have now turned the tables on you, Quark, and beaten you out of every slip and strip. And from the look of things," Odo stretched his finger out to poke nastily at Quark's bare chest, "you've been kind enough to let them have the shirt off your back. How generous of you!"

Quark paced up and down nervously, waving his

arms in agitation; the mauve-colored palm frond
slipped and almost fell. "You raise them, you try to
help them, teach them everything you know—"

"And they turn around and out-Ferengi the Ferengi. So you, too, are discovering the full mental
abilities of our Native friends, eh, Quark? Now that
we've kicked away the crutch of new tech." Odo
threw the sheaf of papers down on the barrelhead.
"Forget your petty losses for a moment. You see this
formative document? It puts to shame the constitutions of every planet in the Federation and, not
incidentally, all my own research on the ideal government. And it was drafted this afternoon by an
eight-year-old child."

The constable shook his head, speaking more to
himself than his audience. "With all the changes
around here, the Natives decided to put together
a workable society to deal with the Cardassian/
Drek'la invasion and the sudden loss of their mag-
ical technology. I helped them a little with some
sociological information and some organizing documents . . . and I get back *this.*"

Constable and Ferengi sighed in unexpected har-
mony, to Odo's chagrin. Quark sat gingerly, holding
the frond carefully to prevent undue financial exposure. "I wonder how Commander Worf is doing?"

After a beat, the Ferengi grinned wickedly. Only
the iron will of Constable Odo prevented him from
doing the same. The image of Commander Worf
trying to "instruct" a class full of inquisitive, socially inept military geniuses raised his spirits ten-
fold.

* * *

Elsewhere on the planet, the Cardassian prisoner, Gul Ragat, walked in front of Julian Bashir like a man already dead whose legs had not yet gotten the message. Jadzia Dax followed somewhere far behind and to the side, so that she and Julian would not drift close enough to make a single target. *I wish we could talk,* thought the doctor. But speech would have informed the prisoner that they were Federation, and Dax wanted to hold that information in reserve.

The Gul had recovered somewhat. The doctor quietly scanned him while he rested and determined that Ragat had no serious injuries—minor burns and abrasions, smoke inhalation, bruises, and other blunt-force trauma, but nothing life-threatening. The diagnosis was a relief. Had Gul Ragat required medical treatment, not all the wild splitheads on Sierra-Bravo 112-II could have stopped Bashir from doing his medical duty, and their cover as "Natives" would have been blown; Ragat would then realize that Starfleet officers had infiltrated the Cardassian/Drek'la occupation.

So what would that mean? wondered Julian; *what's he going to do, publish it in a news clip?* Still, the lovely Jadzia (who had insisted upon command prerogative) had gone to great lengths to guard that secret. The Cardassians and their Drek'la crew evidently believed that the *Defiant* had crashed and burned in the ocean—when in fact it lay submerged in shallow water, intact, under the command of Ensign Joson Wabak and a couple other junior officers, waiting to lift off when the Cardassians and Drek'la were cleansed from orbit. So long as no soldiers of the Empire knew that the *Defiant* still lived, they wouldn't waste time searching for her.

So maybe Jadzia is right after all, Bashir tentatively concluded. Still it was a pain: they couldn't talk for fear the Gul's "universal translator," or whatever the Cardassians called their version, would warn Ragat that Julian and Dax were speaking a Federation, not Native, language. They couldn't show their faces—or even let Ragat look back at them for fear his sharp, Cardassian eyes would penetrate the disguise.

But nothing stopped the Gul himself from talking, which he did without concern for their stony silence. "They couldn't take my title. The house was far too old for that. But they took everything else. Stripped of all rating. No command, no authority, no face. Do you know what it's like to enter a room and hear only silence? I knew Legate Migar and Gul Dukat personally. I was on the list—on the list, I say. I was to be legate, legate! Until . . . *she* came and dashed the cup from my lips. She spilled it on the ground— my honor, my promotion, even my governorship. I was a governor, that's what I tell you. But there were those, those—don't think I didn't know who they were! Neemak, now he was the one to watch. He was the one who waited, any slip, a weakness. And she gave it to him in a silver chalice. She, she, she. Don't mind me—I'm an old man now, I run on. You know what it's like? It's entering a room and hearing all conversation cease, the music, dead silence. Do you know?"

Julian Bashir continued to walk silently behind as they headed toward the hidden skimmer; there was only one left now, the other having long since run out of fuel and been abandoned. The ex-Gul rattled on, an old man with a new, fresh ear for the first time probably in decades. He told them more than they wanted to know about his pain and suffering, his banishment. He never mentioned the name of the woman who had done him wrong (a failed love affair?) save that she was his sister, or perhaps a friend close enough to be called Sister.

Jadzia didn't so much as glance at the prisoner. The doctor felt pangs of guilt. Ragat had made some sort of terrible mistake long ago, something involving a woman, and had been stripped of all his positions and power. No wonder he had fled the Empire and tried to stake out a life far across the quadrant. To a Cardassian, losing face was infinitely worse than losing one's life.

But Bashir and Dax's own problems were more pressing than understanding the enemy: they had to find Captain Sisko and link up. He didn't know that the *Defiant* was still on (actually under) the surface, or that they were waiting for his signal via old-fashioned *radio waves,* which neither the Cardassians nor the vicious, automatic planetary defenses were likely to monitor. Dax, Bashir, and the junior officers back on the ship needed to know what the captain intended, fight or flee; either an attack on the Cardassians and their Drek'la allies or abandonment of the mission would have to be coordinated between Sisko, Dax, and Wabak back on the *Defiant.*

The day was hot and steamy, the ground broken, the sun reflected from brittle crystals in the latinum-laced soil. Gul Ragat fell to his knees without warning, palms loudly slapping the baked mud. The old man had had it for now. But they were near enough the hidden skimmer that they could stop for the night, and mount up and ride in the morning. *If we're chummy enough,* thought the doctor, *I suppose it can carry the three of us.*

Commander Dax caught Julian's eye; she gestured at the ground, then formed a triangle with index fingers and thumbs. The doctor was puzzled for a moment, before he connected the gesture with the stylized image of a tent: they didn't have one, but the idea was clear: *camp here for the night.*

Julian sat down, surprised at how tired he felt. It took even more energy to remain lithe and graceful (*as a genetic freak should,* he added to himself) than merely to march in the bright, red sun. Jadzia, with no reputation to protect, had the easy job.

Gul Ragat continued to talk. He spoke of the invasion of Sierra-Bravo, speaking with repugnance of the "aborigines," how primitive and savage they were, how disgusting, what a perversion of men. His bigotry was bright but blunted by impotence: there was nothing Gul Ragat would ever be able to do about the Natives again, and he knew it. He could curse them freely now, for he was himself free of responsibility: having surrendered to the two of them, he could at last also surrender to his bottled-up rage, humiliation, and prejudice.

After several early attempts by Ragat to turn and look at his captors, the Gul had got the message; he kept his back to the Starfleet officers as he lay on his side, breathing too deeply. Worried, Julian again scanned Ragat from behind. *I'm not sure,* he thought, *but I think some internal bleeding may have started up.* Julian decided that during the night, while Gul Ragat slept, his ghoulish doctor, like a reverse vampire, would slip some life into the old fellow.

The ragged breathing provoked an empathy in Julian Bashir that burned beyond the Hippocratic oath. He gently laid a hand on the Gul's shoulder from behind, squeezing gently.

Ragat cleared his throat. "Thank you," he said. "Good night, doctor."

Alarmed, Julian stared at Dax; but the Trill frowned and shook her head. *Probably just an honorific,* Julian nodded, then lay back to look at the stars.

Just before drifting into a troubled sleep, Gul Ragat raised his voice again to a throaty whisper, which was all he could still manage. "And good night to you too . . . Commander Dax."

Julian grinned, unwilling to look the startled and probably stunned Jadzia Dax in the face. *All that care, the silence, the face masks!* And all along, the damned Cardassian had known exactly who his captors were.

With a quiet chuckle, Julian, too, drifted into the shadowlands, too exhausted even to consider eating.

CHAPTER
2

COMMANDER WORF had his hands full of mayor: he was holding the "mayor-general," Asta-ha, the mother of Tivva-ma, in a pressure hold from which she struggled desperately to escape.

The Klingon was surprised by the female's ingenuity: she independently invented several hold-breaking maneuvers that Worf had not even taught yet. A brilliant pupil! Unfortunately, her lithe but weak body was not up to the level of her tactical brain. Finally, Worf allowed his hold to be broken by Asta-ha's third attempt: creativity in combat must always be encouraged in a student.

"You have progressed adequately," he praised; "but the weakness of your body holds you back. You must reapply yourself to a vigorous calisthenics program until your muscles respond."

Owena-da, a constant irritant, stepped forward.

Worf prepared to bellow the man into silence; but unexpectedly, the Native "tech-master" came to attention and saluted . . . a first for Owena-da. "Sir, request permission to speak freely."

"Request denied. You will use all proper forms of address as you speak." Owena-da already took too many liberties, and Worf was not about to give him more.

"Aye, aye, sir. Sir, this recruit recommends a change in the PT program."

"Oh. You do? I am sure the Klingon Military Command Council will be eager to hear your suggestions."

"Thank you, sir! This recruit has prepared an anatomical kinesthetic analysis of the physical-training regime, sir. Including suggestions for increasing the efficiency and speed of bodily responses through nondestructive hormone therapy." From nowhere, Owena-da pulled a sheaf of *paper,* which the villagers had lately invented. From where Worf stood, he could see that it was covered with a dense thicket of crabbed writing in the language used by Starfleet—a language the Natives had learned in five days.

The Klingon sighed, accepting the pages and handwaving Owena-da back into the ranks. Worf did not look at the paper . . . not yet. "On your faces," he said quietly, but with absolute authority.

The Natives dropped quickly to the standard push-up position. "Down, up," began Worf; "down, up, down, up, down, up . . . *halfway down.*" Worf held them halfway through a single push-up, waiting until he heard groans and saw them beginning to collapse before resuming the count.

An hour later, safely ensconced in his makeshift bivouac tent, the Klingon read through Owena-da's analysis with mounting irritation and frustration. He keenly felt the slap to his authority—a raw recruit, telling Worf of House Mogh how to teach physical training! It was a deadly insult to his military bearing, his honor, and his house. And the most humiliating factor was that Worf would have to implement Owena-da's training recommendations immediately, because they were brilliant and insightful and training time was horribly short.

Worf brooded for too long after finishing the paper. Honor dictated that he would even have to submit the paper to the Federation journal for immediate adoption throughout Starfleet and the civilian milieu.

And Worf's honorable role in defending Sierra-Bravo against the Cardassian/Drek'la invasion would forever be subsumed under the Natives' miraculous tactical and training innovations. For generations, their genius had been blocked by instant access to all the "new tech" their hearts desired. Now, under the stress of having to fend for their own lives, the native intellectual capacity was bursting forth like the human war goddess Athena erupting from the head of Zeus in Worf's favorite human myth, taught him by his foster father.

And who would draw the lesson for the Federation itself? "And who was it who warned of this danger?" he asked aloud; the wind supplied no answer. Nobody would remember. Worf's honor had been snatched by Klingon thieves, won back at enormous cost . . . and now was about to be buried under the casual brilliance of a race of supergenius dilettantes.

The situation was intolerable. But Worf was a Klingon, and had a duty to perform, so the intolerable would be tolerated. He rose; the squadron would have set up their spring traps by now, ready to be tested. The Klingon grimaced as he ducked through the tent flap, dreading the marvelous innovations in booby trapping he was about to see.

Major Kira lay on the deck on Level Four, held prone by a heavy foot planted on her cervical vertibrae. She made no attempt to struggle; she already knew it would be useless. *Of course, the whole damned thing is useless, isn't it?* Through overlong familiarity, the thought barely bothered her anymore.

She listened at the corner of her ear to the dean: "You are not worthy of trust. You must be restrained. You will wear the collar of slaves."

The Kai's voice sounded offstage, faintly chastising without provoking. "As you were restrained by the Dominion?"

A long silence. "Yes, as we were."

"I see." Kai Winn's tone would have chilled a winter river.

Kira, however, could hardly imagine caring less than she did at that moment. The station was lost. The brave Bajorans had accepted surrender. Even the vaunted Federation was stymied . . . there had been no further reaction to the seizure of *Deep Space*

Nine. She was yanked to her feet and held immobile, while a binding plastic collar was locked onto her throat.

Bitterness tasted sweet on her tongue. Kira stood when they released her, not even glancing at the piece of catwalk railing she had battered over the dean's head, striking from ambush with every Newton of force she could gather. The power of the blow had knocked him to his knobby knees, but that was the only effect; when he stood up, he was unhurt.

"You must receive a demonstration of the power of the collar of slaves," recited the dean, his curiously uninflected voice nevertheless conveying a subterranean river of emotion. He made no overt signal, but the collar tightened, cutting off Kira's windpipe.

They had caught her after an exhalation. Within seconds, her lungs screamed for air. But she stood absolutely still, eyes closed, not letting herself gasp or double over and keeping her hands at her side. The collar tightened further, and Kira felt consciousness ebb. *Cutting off blood to my brain,* she thought dully.

She felt a sharp pressure against her cheek, but it didn't seem important; the blackness welcomed her. Then her head ached, suddenly washed with agony. She was drowning in a lake, coughing up bitter-tasting water onto what must have been the seashore. But the beach felt too hard, too cold.

She lay on the deck of maintenance tube 19, Level Four, while a pair of insectoid invaders sprayed bitter-tasting water on her face. "You now see the authority of the collar for slaves," buzzed the dean.

"You must obey the rules for prisoners or the collar will be used to execute you. There is a limbic integrator. It senses violent impulses and acts automatically."

The offstage voice again, surely the Kai's. She was speaking to someone, one of her special team. "How are you coming with the project I set for you, finding the Orb?"

"We are nearly done, my Kai," said a man whom Kira vaguely recognized from Ops duty during the initial battle.

"You will finish in time?"

"We will."

"As I instructed, you will tell me when you find where the rebels hid the Orb, and I will send Kira to fetch it." It seemed odd for the Kai to emphasize the first three words, but Kira had other needs.

Dimly, she sought the anxious figure of Kai Winn. *How curiously motherlike she looks!* "Was I—unconscious?" croaked Major Kira.

"Yes, child. I think the collar cut off the flow of blood through the artery." The Kai leaned close, speaking for Kira's ears only—though Kira presumed that the insectoids heard every word, either using audio-amps or because they had exceptionally keen hearing. "There is a time when we who walk with the Prophets must learn that humility is an important virtue. Trust me, child. I surely know what I'm speaking about. It seems the end of the world, but really, it's not: what you can tolerate, you can endure."

The major's lips flickered for a momentary smile. *The words from the psalm: tolerate and endure.* "I will struggle no longer," said Kira Nerys. "You will watch me become a model slave." She allowed herself to be led in purest docility back to the access corridor.

A model slave . . . and astonished, Kira realized that she meant it. The insects had taken over the station, and there was nothing that anyone could do about it. *Not yet,* she appended dully. Struggle was futile; she proved it to herself alone in her cabin, deliberately working herself into a fury, only to feel the collar tighten by itself as it had on the dean's command.

"I'm just trying to lull them into a false security," she told herself; but it was hard to believe it. Many times over the next days, she "woke" to realize she had been serving the dean and the other invaders for several hours without noting a single, militarily useful weakness, nothing to use against the enemy. *Do I slip so easily into a slave's role?* she wondered, lying awake in terror half through the night.

She caught the Kai watching her through lazily lidded eyes, a knowing smile on Winn's lips. Kira felt the seduction of acceptance, and the thrill it produced set her body to shivering. *How deep into this "cover" can I go and still escape?*

"What will you do during this Resistance, child?" asked Kai Winn unexpectedly the next afternoon.

"Resist," said Kira, hearing the echo of a previous conversation. But she meant she would *resist temptation* to succumb to her fate. *Prophets,* she prayed, *it's so damned easy to make a big show and resist, defiant, like a teenage girl in Shakar's cell during the Occupation.* She bent, lowering her head as the dean approached; she waited for him to issue orders . . . they were never difficult or humiliating, which made it worse. *But it's a hell of a lot harder to resist with bowed head and a soft voice. Help me! Don't let me lose my temper or lose myself!* If the Prophets answered, Kira couldn't hear Their words.

Kira's duties were to run messages to the Kai and other Bajorans, demonstrate the use of station controls (the dean never asked Major Kira about weaponry), reprogram the replicators, and bring the ceremonial first and last meals to the dean (though he served himself, for which Kira thanked the Prophets). She was to finish each task and return to the dean, unless he contacted her over the comsystem to give further orders. But Kira perfected the art of dawdling, which she'd never mastered before, taking as long to complete each project as she could reasonably pretend to need. She walked slowly, in a stately manner, killing even more time: every ten minutes slain was one fewer task before she could crawl into her rack.

Kira Nerys shrank and shrank, until at last she found her irreducible core. Her spirits contracted into a sharp ice-blade that pricked her breast and irritated her stomach. After the rest of her pride, efficiency, courage, recklessness, and bravado had boiled away, Major Kira found at last the pure will that would finally drive away the new invaders. And she found a new respect for Kai Winn, whose own will must have been mighty indeed to sustain her through so many years of silent, hidden resistance— with a bowed head and a soft voice.

Kira's eyes began to open. She began to see every

crack and weakness, every overlooked line of attack in the invaders' profile. Their sleep was too sound, almost comatose. When eating, they neither talked nor looked around. They needed special suits outside the hull to withstand cosmic background radiation. The "insects" were too individualistic, tending to go wildsiding through the station, and the dean could hardly reel them in at times. They were nevertheless terrified to be alone and always roamed at least by threes.

Kira easily accepted that they had been Dominion slaves, probably as completely dominated as the Jem'Hadar. But they had been used for other purposes, and Kira probed to discover what exactly they'd done for the Founders (while she bowed and answered, "Yes, most gracious dean; instantly, great one"). The Founders, Kira knew from personal experience and conversations with her friend Odo, liked specialization. They used the Jem'Hadar for war and the Vorta for diplomacy; what could the Liberated do for shapeshifters?

One curious incident puzzled Kira, and she fretted endlessly about what it could mean. It occurred early in the occupation of—of *Emissary's Sanctuary,* two days after the dean and his crew seized control.

At first, Kira made a point not even to mention Keiko, Jake, and the other children and civilians in the eight bombardment shelters around the main Promenade level. She still hoped, absurdly, that the occupation would be brief, and Keiko and the kids could come out after a few days. Keiko played her part well: she laid low, as she would have said, neither communicating nor trying to leave, doing nothing to reveal her presence.

But after several hours, the dean stopped and "stared" at Kira. In fact, she had to infer the stare, since his face was a featureless mask. "There are beings not accounted for in the inventory," he said, his actual voice behind the universal translator sounding so disturbingly like the shellclickers of Bajor that Kira shuddered.

"I don't know what you mean." She was still in her sullen phase then, and in no mood to cooperate.

"Our scans reveal there are 237 beings in this enclosed environment who are not listed on the prisoner manifest you gave us. You must find them and return them to their places."

Kira said nothing. She was well aware that the aliens would swiftly locate the other "prisoners," but that didn't mean she had to help. But Kai Winn answered in Kira's place. "My friends, the rest of the personnel are in the shelters on this level." The Kai gestured around her; she was standing directly in front of the Klingon restaurant, which was across the circular hallway from one of those very shelters. Winn turned and pointed at it. "There are eight of these structures. The rest of the . . . the residents here are secured inside."

Kira had a momentary urge to leap the distance and break Kai Winn's nose. But she pressed her lips together and said nothing, contenting herself with a look that should have frozen the marrow in the old woman's bones.

"They are secured?" repeated the dean.

"Yes, my most gracious host. They are safe."

The dean turned away. Kira heard no words, but an alien moved to stand in front of Bombardment Shelter Six as if guarding it from attack. Looking along the Promenade in both directions, the major saw that guards were taking up positions in front of alternate shelters. But since they made no effort to enter, Kira slowly forgot about it. Keiko seemed safe—for the moment.

Several more times, Kai Winn asked one lieutenant or another as the occupation progressed about the "special project," which evidently was to find the Orb. *How odd,* thought the major; *how could she possibly not know where it's hidden?* It was inconceivable that the Kai would not be able to put her finger-ends on the Orb at a moment's notice. But seemingly, those she sent to hide it had succeeded beyond anyone's wildest imagination. *Buying time? Does she still hope for rescue from the Federation?*

Two days passed, and Kira began to worry, however. The last time she had talked with the botanist, Keiko had promised to stay secured for two or three days. But how long could she wait? Clearly, the aliens were not leaving anytime soon.

They continued their sentrylike marching up and down the Promenade, looking like military beetles on parade. Every time Kira shuffled through the Promenade, she felt a little more nervous about what would happen when somebody, Keiko or one of the other civilians in a shelter, decided to go stir-crazy and break out.

She didn't have long to wait. The first casualty of claustrophobia was not Keiko; it was Jounda Mar, an archeologist from the Riis Valley on Bajor. At last, Jounda couldn't take the isolation—she was in a shelter with only twelve people counting herself—and she cracked the seal and yanked open the door. Major Kira, slave collar now in place, was attending the dean while he sampled food from a Bajoran noodle house. "Attending" in this case meant sitting next to him, eating whatever dish he ate first to make sure it wasn't poisoned.

When the door to Shelter Two popped, hissed, and swung open, and Jounda stepped outside trembling, the dean's reaction was so startling that Kira dropped a plate full of *malibon* on the deck, where it shattered. The alien leapt to his feet with such alacrity that he knocked over the table, clenched his fist (which Kira had determined activated his com circuit), and began shouting "Emergency, emergency, breakout on Deck Nine!"

The aliens swarmed the location, led by the dean himself, and they pulled the door all the way open and mobbed the shelter. Jounda screamed once, but then she fell bitterly silent.

Kira rushed over to mediate, to prevent the aliens from panicking or the Bajoran civilians from putting up a futile resistance that would only get someone hurt. *Prophets,* she thought, *I'm turning into Kai Winn!* Jounda's once-white jumper was stained with two days of grime and sweat, and the dozen of them smelled like they hadn't bathed, naturally enough. Kira was shocked to see how quickly the civilians fell right back into their "occupation daze," obeying the aliens' gestures and incomprehensible commands—for none of the civilians had a universal translator, of course.

"My lord," said Kira, pushing herself in between the dean and Jounda; "don't let your anger get the better of your judgment. These people are civilians, not warriors—they pose no risk to you!"

But the dean paid her no attention, merely pulling her aside gently. "Replace them," he said to his men, "quickly, lest we lose one or more than one."

And while Kira stared, stupified, the aliens proceeded to return the civilians to the bombardment shelter. Jounda Mar's pleas were in vain, and neither would the dean listen to Kira. "You don't need to put them back!" shouted the major. "They won't attack you—they're as trustworthy as the rest of us." She was uncomfortably aware that that, actually, was saying a lot: when shove had come to tumble, the grand, independent, passionate Bajorans on *Emissary's Sanctuary* had become as docile as a herd of curlbeasts.

But it made no difference. Without even listening, the aliens returned Jounda Mar and the other eleven civilians to Bombardment Shelter Two and resealed it. And there they stayed.

Over the next two days, there were similar "breakouts" from each of the other shelters. Jake's was next to try to leave, followed by the other six: three the same day, then two more the next, then the last, Shelter Five, containing forty-one assorted civil servants brought up to the station by the Kai. The aliens' behavior was identical in every case: they treated the incidents like a prisoner breakout, swarming the "escapees" and returning them forcibly to their "cells."

Kira understood why: somehow, the dean had got

it into his carapace that the civilians hiding in the shelters were *prisoners* confined involuntarily to cells, and he chose, for whatever reason, to continue their sentences. *But why? What had made him think that?* Kira shook her head, still not understanding when the final secretary was pushed into the last shelter already full of Kai Winn's bureaucrats, a fate almost worse than death. A thought tickled Kira's hindbrain: for some reason, she knew that this was an important—even critical—piece of information, if she could only figure out the reason for the aberrant behavior.

Why? Why would they make such an absurd mistake? But the Prophets, Who knew all, chose not to whisper in the major's ear, and she remained in ignorance.

Lieutenant Commander Jadzia Dax was awake before the sun, pacing in the chilly predawn, developing a plan. When she glanced at Gul Ragat, she was startled to find him watching her, his black Cardassian eyes enigmatic but hard. Julian had not yet stirred.

Ragat sat up, pulling his rough blanket around his frail body. His trapezius muscles, stretching from neck to shoulder tips—huge and powerful on most Cardassians—were instead thin and limp, sagging pathetically; the bony ridges surrounding his eye sockets were dark gray, and his dull eyes were sunken into deep flesh.

"I didn't expect you to wake for another couple of hours," said Dax. The charade was over; Ragat knew who the both of them were, Bashir and Dax.

"Old men don't sleep well," he said, shrugging. "Even those of us made old long before our time by betrayal and dishonor."

"What tipped you?"

At first, the Gul simply smiled, dark and mysterious, like Garak telling lunchroom tales to the doctor. Then Ragat slumped, letting his head sink. He tried a self-deprecating smile. "You swore when you couldn't shoot me. You said 'oh, hell.' The aborigines don't have any concept of heaven or hell. So you were Federation—Starfleet."

"From that you knew our names?"

Ragat looked up at her. "We knew only one Starfleet ship in orbit around this planet, the *U.S.S. Defiant.* With all the trouble our two peoples have had, you'd imagine we would make an effort to memorize the crew manifests of ships we're likely to encounter. Wouldn't you?"

Dax said nothing.

"You are a high-ranking female. You certainly weren't Major Kira; I can smell Bajorans. So I took the chance that you were the Trill."

Jadzia cocked her head at Bashir and raised an eyebrow.

Ragat snorted, sounding almost like their own Constable Odo. "Who else but Julian Bashir would be sneaking behind me with a medical tricorder?"

Dax nodded. "Anything else we should know?" She leaned close. "Any reason I shouldn't kill you now, before Julian wakes up?"

He blanched, turning his face away. "The best reason in the quadrant: I know something you need to know but don't."

"That being?"

"I know the story of the aborigines. How they got here, why they have such technology but are so primitive and uncivilized."

"Why?"

The Gul shook his head slowly, wincing at the pain. "Release me to my men and I'll tell you what you need to know."

"Tell me what I want to know, and I won't release you from this life."

For an instant, Dax was sure she saw terror flicker across the Gul's face. *He's a man used to living in fear,* she intuited. Then the Cardassian mask fell across it once more. "We, ah, appear to be at an impasse, Commander. Will you kill me before even finding out what information I hold?"

She stood straight and contemplated the prostrate form for a beat. "No. I won't. Not yet, anyway."

Bashir awoke.

Gul Ragat struggled to his feet and picked up his pack in weary resignation. "Don't look so tortured," she said, feeling little pity but much repugnance. "You don't have to walk. We have transportation." The Gul relaxed visibly, and Dax was sorry she had told him so quickly.

She stared at his back as he waited. *He does know something,* she concluded. *At the least, he's found electronic or even paper records. If it's a main computer, then maybe we can reprogram the planetary defenses to let the Defiant pass!*

It was a charming thought—whose reality depended on nothing but the whim of an ancient Cardassian Gul, unusually cynical and manipulative even for that species. *Or is he really that old, chronologically?* She shrugged; he was ancient in mind if not in body. Jadzia Dax throttled back her racing thoughts and began scooping her belongings into a pack. At least, considering Gul Ragat's condition, he wouldn't be making any quick breaks for the border.

33

CHAPTER
3

CAPTAIN BENJAMIN SISKO stayed unobtrusive, leaving day-to-day contacts between Federation and Natives to the other away-team members. He tried to perfect his own antitoxin, and it got better. *Still, I don't know how much longer we can last,* he thought, hypospraying himself with the latest experiment.

Captain Sisko was particularly pleased at the progress Commander Worf was making on the military side and with Chief O'Brien's work with Owena-da to develop home-grown "new tech" to replace the fantastic devices the Natives had relied on for millenia, but that no longer worked. *They don't work anymore because I stopped them,* he thought for the thousandth time. No matter what the others imagined, Sisko was increasingly aware that making such a terrible decision—cutting off all power to the northern hemisphere—didn't get easier with time. He still stewed over the dilemma, second-guessing everything he had done.

He took a deep breath. Some of the ache was gone. The new serum did in fact work marginally better.

"They are learning," he told O'Brien, injecting the chief; "but are they learning quickly enough? Will we be able to repulse the next Cardassian attack?"

"I think it likely," said O'Brien, who continued to cough. Sisko couldn't tell yet whether he had improved. *Of course, he'll say he has, regardless,* realized the captain.

"Spears and arrows against disruptors?"

"People confuse not being state-of-the-art with being obsolete," said O'Brien; "especially us engineers. But you know, old-fashioned radio still works as good as subspace over short distances; and you can die just as easily from an arrow in the gut today as you could two thousand years ago, sir."

Sisko stroked his chin, looking at the three wood-plus-local-steel devices the chief had placed before him on a fallen, blue-gray log. Owena-da's first design was what O'Brien had called an "arbalest" but looked to Sisko like a crossbow, a "steel" archer's bow mounted on a shaft, with a trigger to loosen the string. The second, invented the next day during lunch by Colonel-Mayor Asta-ha (cut down from mayor-general) was a pair of miniature, hand-held, angled catapults, each of which fired a small, cast-metal ball split in half, the two halves connected by a two-meter length of cable: after firing, the halves of each ball would separate, pulling the cable taut, and rotate at a high speed, wrapping around the legs and arms of anyone unlucky enough to be standing in the way. *A two-shot, automatic bola pistol,* thought Sisko, awed.

The third device, also by Owena-da, was more complex, a technological leap in two days that had taken humans a thousand years. The weapon resembled a tube with a trio of metal bulbs growing out the rear end. Cocking the device by operating a pump lever several times compressed the air in the bulbs; the compressed air then fired a needle-sharp poison dart that O'Brien estimated could pierce Cardassian battle armor in a square shot within twenty meters range. Owena-da dubbed it the "Viper's Kiss" (at least that's how the universal translator rendered the name).

As Sisko gingerly fingered the Viper's Kiss, he heard a dull explosion outside and down the hillock to the east, in the area Worf and O'Brien had selected as a munitions proving ground. The colonel-mayor, her daughter Tivva-ma, and Owena-da were experimenting with the Sierra-Bravo version of gunpowder, though they hadn't yet learned to control the gas expansion. The Captain shuddered slightly; *have I built a Frankenstein's monster?* On whom would the erstwhile Tiffnakis, now called Vanimastavvi, turn once they had rid their planet of its Cardassian infestation?

As least O'Brien had stopped hacking, and his color looked better. The captain was encouraged.

"Chief," he said, "could you ask the rest of the away team to step into my tent?" While O'Brien beetled away, Sisko paced, hands clasped behind his back, trying to frame his argument. "Gentlemen," he greeted the team when they arrived, injecting each man except Odo. "We are in a tricky situation here. All . . . *this.*" Sisko gestured expansively, indicating the Vanimastavvi all around them.

Everyone seemed to understand what he meant. "The Natives are progressing much faster than any of us expected," said Worf.

"I told you about the constitution," said Constable Odo, visibly piqued. "If you ask me, they're moving *too* fast."

"You're right. The question is what to do about them."

"By the time they finish," bragged O'Brien with a wicked grin, "they'll have such weapons, the damned Cardassian bastards won't know what hit 'em!"

"I want my clothes back," insisted Quark in a quiet, angry voice. He looked particularly oafish wearing animal skins and wooden clogs.

"Gentlemen, we are in the fight of our lives here. The *Defiant* is gone, and who knows when it will return. Our food supplies are dwindling, and we still can't eat the native plants or animals."

"Sir," interrupted Chief O'Brien, "maybe we can get the Tiffnakis, or whatever they're calling themselves now, maybe we can get them to invent a food reprocessor?"

Odo snorted. "Oh be serious, Chief. They don't even know the first thing about food chemistry. All the intelligence in the quadrant can't turn lead into latinum!"

"Why don't we let them read a Federation chemistry textbook?"

"Did you happen to bring one along, Chief?

Captain, can you please continue?" Odo turned his back on the chief and folded his arms defiantly.

Sisko had kept quiet during the exchange, using his lack of interest to make the point to O'Brien. "Thank you, Constable. We must raid the Cardassians again. They have the only food we can eat, the only water we can drink. I'm tempted to take the Vanimastavvi on the raid, or allow them to perform it themselves."

"May I interrupt, Captain?" Without waiting for a response, Worf turned to face the entire group and continued. "I do not advise that we raid the Cardassians."

"How are we supposed to eat?" demanded Chief O'Brien, who was beginning to look a little thin and stretched, thought Sisko.

"Up until now," said the Klingon, "the Cardassians have been entirely on the offensive. They may be aware that the power is offline, if they have attempted to use captured native technology. But they will not associate that with the passive, ah, Natives." Worf paused, waiting for response.

Sisko nodded. "We're listening, Commander."

"The Cardassians have attacked many Native villages. In every case, the Natives have responded with panic and ill-prepared and ineffective defenses, allowing themselves to be overwhelmed in a matter of moments."

"Worf," snapped O'Brien, holding his stomach, "we already know all that."

"But as soon as the Natives go on the offensive, especially if they are effective, the Cardassians will be alerted to the changed situation. They will respond. Although they are not Klingons, they are still determined and clever warriors. We do not want merely to bloody their noses. If we are going to tip our hands, we must do so decisively."

"Never do your enemy a *small* injury," quoted Sisko.

"That is well said, sir. You raise his ire but do not cause him to fear you."

"I take it you are suggesting, Mr. Worf, that instead of a small raid, we launch a war."

"That is what I recommend as chief military advisor."

"Does anybody disagree? Gentlemen?"

Odo frowned, opened his mouth, but closed it again. O'Brien didn't respond. But Quark cleared his throat.

"May I say something, Captain?"

"We already know you want your clothing back, Quark," said the constable.

"Mr. Worf, Mr. O'Brien," said the captain, "Begin preparing plans for a full-strength assault on the Cardassians. Odo, go aloft as a local bird and scout out where the biggest body of invaders lies. And Quark. . . ." Sisko hesitated, finally turning to look at his troops. The Ferengi was good at negotiations—but tactical planning for a military operation?

"Mr. Quark, why don't you go: bargain for your clothes back. Team dismissed; I have reports to begin drafting." *And many dark and frightening thoughts to explore,* he added to himself.

* * *

Dax sat in the shade watching Gul Ragat, the beat-up skimmer parked beneath a scrubby blue tree. He stood rigidly in the high sunlight, stiff as a board, hands clasped behind his back in a motion that would have looked regal on a fellow not wearing rags.

"Gul Ragat," said Bashir, "get into some shade, for heaven's sake. We have water—Cardassian water."

"I do not require water," said the Gul. "Thank you, Doctor."

Dax smiled. She closed her eyes, resting. "Mad dogs and Cardassians go out in the midday sun," she said, more to herself than to Bashir.

"Why does that sound familiar?" asked the doctor anyway. "I'm sure I've heard. . . ." He trailed off in silence, for Dax wasn't listening.

She pondered Ragat's offer: information for freedom. Fundamentally, it was a good trade. *The last thing in the world I want is to be dragging a prisoner around with me, especially a frail, young-old man.* But there was the problem that Ragat knew who they were, which so far the rest of the Cardassians did not. She relied on that ignorance. If the Cardassians realized there was a Starfleet away team on Sierra Bravo, they would move mountains to hunt them down and kill or capture them all. *We're their only natural predators,* she said to herself.

"Julian," she said in a voice almost too soft for him to hear, even sitting next to her. "If we can figure a way to keep Ragat off the board for the next week or so, I see no reason not to let him go."

"I was just thinking the same," said Bashir. "If

40

he's telling the truth about the information, that might be much more beneficial to us than a prisoner."

"I doubt the Cardassians would trade much for his carcass. To hear him talk, there won't be too many statues erected to Gul Ragat on Cardassia Prime."

"His troops seem loyal," said Bashir, but he sounded dubious even as he said it.

"His troops are a bunch of renegade brigands. His XO would probably pop the cork on some expensive Cardassian Champagne—if there is such a thing—if we told him Ragat was a prisoner."

Bashir nodded. "Then let's accept his offer."

"We can dump him in the wilderness," suggested Dax.

"*With* water and provisions," said the doctor, giving Dax a hard look.

"Of course. Enough for a couple of weeks . . . easily long enough to hike back to a Cardassian encampment, if he doesn't get lost."

"As you say," said Bashir, still sounding as though he were trying to convince himself rather than Dax, "the information is more valuable than the man."

"If," said Dax, "he's telling us the truth."

Gul Ragat turned to stare directly at the pair. "Of course he's telling you the truth," said the Cardassian. "We came across a nodule that I believe is a terminal of some sort, connecting directly with the main planetary computers, wherever they are. We have been able to access part of it . . . the historical records."

Dax fell silent in astonishment. Beside her, Bashir

was likewise speechless. "You really have it?" she said, quite unable to keep the eagerness out of her voice.

Ragat sighed, stepping into the shadows at last. He was sweating, Dax noticed, a strange, bluish perspiration, whether natural for a Cardassian or from the planet, she wasn't sure. "I will take you to my glorious imperial camp," he said with lip curled. "You will be able to query the computer yourself. We can also reprovision there. I want *four* weeks worth of rations—in case I *do* get lost."

"How many guards?" asked the Trill, warily.

"But two," said Ragat. "Not recognizing your presence, I took all but two junior noncoms out on the Wild Hunt." The bitterness in his voice almost made Dax feel pity. Then she remembered the butchered village, and she pressed her lips together to hold back the fury. "Yes," continued Ragat, "we had just left the camp when you attacked us. It's no more than, um, four or five of your kilometers distant."

Dax leapt to her feet, so eager to see this alien computer "nodule" that she couldn't bear to rest any longer. "Lead on," she commanded. Anticipation all but drove the rage from her mind . . . until later. Until it would be needed.

Bashir groaned. "Jadzia, that's—"

She held up her hand, stopping his objection. "Yes, Julian, I already know that's not the line from the play. Let's get across this damned gully and find that deserted encampment. We'll leave the skimmer here," she added as afterthought; "your engines are so damned noisy, it would be like calling ahead for an appointment." They set out across the sand, trekking toward their rendezvous with an alien brain.

Deserted the camp was indeed. In fact, Dax was quite astonished to discover the Gul had told the truth: there were only two Cardassian guards at home; one was relaxing out of sight, suggested Ragat. "Julian," said Dax, "take care of the sentry."

Bashir took down the sentry with no muss, a single shot on stun laying him gently to the dirt. The three-man team approached silently, ghosting up to the fallen enemy. "What now, Jadzia?" asked the doctor. He frowned, starting to dig in his heels.

"No need," said Dax, holding up her hand.

"The liquor ruse again?"

She shook her head. "Nobody would believe it a second time. But I have another brainstorm. Julian, can you inject something into his heel that will cause his foot to swell up and itch?"

"Itch? How much?"

"A lot."

"And *why?* You don't think he's going to tell us anything in exchange for the antidote, do you?"

Dax laughed. "Come on, what could a corporal possibly tell us? Do you think Gul Ragat confides in his noncoms?" The Gul affected not to hear the reference, and Dax continued. "But when he comes to and tries to figure out what happened, if he finds what looks like a weird bug-bite, don't you think he'll put two and two together?"

Bashir smiled. "All right, Jadzia; one itchy bee-sting coming up."

While the doctor mixed the potion, Dax scouted the compound with Gul Ragat in tow. "If you make a sound," she promised, "it will be your last. There's no Julian Bashir here now to get in the way." She looked significantly at the Gul, who swallowed and tried to look nonchalant. But she could see he was shaken. He knew, of course, how many lives she had lived—and that some of her incarnations had been rather more bloodthirsty than the typical Starfleet officer's. Gul Ragat said not a word as they crept up on the remaining guard.

They caught him sleeping on a couch, a regs manual lying open on his chest. He snored lustily, obviously out for some time. Dax returned to Bashir, who had just finished anointing the unconscious guard's foot. She dragged the doctor into the library, where he hyposprayed the sleeping guard with a sedative that would keep him out for three hours or more. "He's already asleep," said Dax. "He'll just assume he was tired."

Gul Ragat snorted, sounding almost like Constable Odo. "How clever you can be," he said, nodding approval. "I see your long contact with the Empire has rubbed off on you."

"Computer," said Dax, all seriousness again. Try as she might, she couldn't get the image of the Native massacre out of her brain. Nothing Ragat said seemed at all cute or witty when superimposed as voice-over to that internal video feed.

The Cardassian curled his lip as if smelling something distasteful. "Of course. Let's get down to business."

CHAPTER
4

DAX MADE RAGAT walk in front along the corridor and kept a phaser trained on his back. She trusted that her own reactions would be faster than the old man's, even if he had a head start from plotting beforehand: he wouldn't elude them or sound any sort of alarm. Bashir searched all about them with his medical scanner, looking for life signs; Cardassian, Native, or anything else.

But the Gul was in no mood to fight. Looking terribly bent over, like a question mark, as if he really were old—but he wasn't!—he padded through the prefabricated corridors that had been thrown up in a day by the Cardassian Corps of Engineers, and led them to a steel door secured by a complex lock. Dax examined it closely, saying, "Julian, I think even Chief O'Brien would have trouble bypassing this security protocol."

She caught hold of Gul Ragat's arm and pulled him to the lock. "You'd better be able to open this, if you want to live to rejoin your friends."

"Don't look at me for relief," said Bashir, as the Gul flicked his eyes at the doctor. "I'm not in command here." *Julian doesn't look pleased,* thought Dax. *He doesn't like the whole hostage game. Well, hell—neither do I.*

But Gul Ragat at least understood the rules. With a great sigh, as if leaping a threshhold he never thought he would cross, he poked and beeped the touchpad until the door reluctantly ground open.

Air hissed around the edges as the seal cracked. Dax sniffed as they entered: she smelled not only ozone but the curiously wet and fresh smell of cold nitrogen, quickly replaced by Sierra-Bravo's metallic atmosphere. Her eyes were immediately caught by the alien nodule . . . *an apt description,* she thought. It was a silvery ball, much smaller than she expected, no larger than her fist. It floated in an antigrav field, or else it generated its own.

The Cardassians had surrounded it with a dizzy collection of dish antennas and electronic probes—none actually touching the nodule, but arrayed around it in a meter-wide sphere. The Gul crossed to the nearest console and screen, ignoring the nodule itself. He touched a single control, and the screen flickered to life.

It was filled from edge to edge by Cardassian block lettering. Bashir leaned close, reading as best he could, while Dax kept her eye on Ragat. Surrounded by as much equipment as was in that room, she was nervous lest he activate some sort of alarm, causing an entire regiment to beam into the compound from one of the ships in orbit.

She glanced at Bashir: the doctor was so engrossed with what he was reading, he had completely forgotten everything else in the room. His mouth stood open in astonishment. At last, he came to some sort of end. He pressed the screen-down button several times, then stepped back, shaking his head and blinking moisture back into his irritated eyes.

"Well," he said, his voice soft and shaken, "I guess that answers a few questions."

"What is it, Julian?"

Twice, Bashir started to respond, then closed his mouth again and thought. The third time, he made it. "Jadzia—Commander—you weren't too far off in some of your speculations." His lips were evidently too dry; he licked them, but it didn't seem to do much good.

"Yes?" she said, revolving her hand as if to say *speed it up!*

"Jadzia . . . this entire planet is a gigantic social-science experiment."

An icy, invisible fist gripped at the commander's bowels. "Conducted by whom? To discover what?"

Julian Bashir sat on a blue chair, stroking the console and thinking. "A long time ago—that seven-million-year timeline you calculated for the hut hit it on the head—the Natives' ancestors grew interested in the question of whether technology and society were inseparable. So they . . . God, this is so horrific. They found a planet amenable to their biology and terraformed it—I suppose they also genetically engineered the animals for consciousness and intelligence, but the scraps I read weren't clear on that point. Maybe that's natural for those animals on the Natives' home system, Native Prime I guess you can call it."

Dax waited. "Julian, are you going to tell me? Or do I have to learn Cardassian and wait for the novel?"

"All right. They sprinkled the planet surface with a random sample of their technology, which was far in advance of our own. Then they raised about a *hundred million* of their own children in complete isolation from any adults, any elements of culture or society, even from the language the Native Primes themselves spoke."

Nobody said a word; a solid minute of silence passed, punctuated by the clicks and hisses of the Cardassian air recirculators. "God is the right word," said Dax at last. "That's exactly what the Native Primes were playing. And a bored and decadent God at that."

"Then they took these kids—"

"I can guess the rest, Julian. The Native Primes took the kids, as soon as they could walk, and transported them down to the surface of Sierra-Bravo, all alone—no mother, no father, no culture, no community, nothing but each other and a world filled with enough 'new tech' to allow some of the kids to survive. Julian, what was the death rate?"

He shrugged. "Well, there were a hundred million to start, and today, seven million years later, the population appears stable at eleven million. I would guess that most of the deaths occurred within the first year."

Dax felt nauseated. "That's a death rate of 89 percent of *their own children*. And they let the experiment continue!"

"They surrounded the planet with defenses intended to keep everyone away. I suppose the Native Primes must have died out or lost interest millions of years ago, but they never terminated the experiment as long as they lived. The eleven million Natives left on Sierra-Bravo probably wouldn't be enough to be self-sustaining, except for the technology that provides food, shelter, clothing, entertainment, and everything else they need."

"Julian, I hope you're wrong, dead wrong about that."

"About what?"

"That the Natives won't be self-sustaining, now that we've . . ." She didn't need to finish. She was sure Bashir understood the catastrophic, unlivable guilt they would all feel if a ham-fisted attempt to save the Natives ended up killing them all instead. *Eleven million ghosts dragging me to my grave. Could I ever live with myself?* She fought down existential terror. Even three centuries of life hadn't prepared her to shoulder such a weight of culpability.

Bashir's face paled. "Here's to being dead wrong," he toasted, raising an imaginary glass.

"Well," said Dax, still trembling, "I guess they proved one point."

"They did?"

"Civilization and technology *are* separable." She

laughed, more from nervousness than mirth. The cold metal computer banks surrounding her looked so much like *Deep Space Nine,* she felt a great longing to get the hell off the planet and back home—a home she would probably never see again, now that Kai Winn had her clutches on it. "I guess Worf was right after all, all those warnings he gave about technology not being enough to sustain a society."

Bashir shrugged; he didn't seem interested in Worf's philosophy of technology. "So now what?" he asked.

"Well, it eliminates one worry." She paused. "At least we don't have to fret about violating the Prime Directive. There *is no* natural evolution to disturb in this demonic social experiment." She stepped forward, taking Gul Ragat's arm. "Okay, you gave what you promised. Let's get on the hump. We've got some flying to do." Somehow, the bloody crimes of Gul Ragat didn't seem so significant to Dax at the moment, against this new landscape.

Then they left, Ragat shutting and sealing the door behind them. They exited the way they had come, hiking the three klicks back to the remaining skimmer. Again, they sandwiched Gul Ragat between the two of them, Dax driving, and set off across the desert.

The landscape below shimmered in the heat-induced turbulence. Dax was quiet for the moment, thinking about the Native Primes, the children, the experiment. At last she spoke. "I'm going to dump him off about a hundred and fifty kilometers from the nearest Cardassian base," she shouted over her shoulder.

Bashir nodded, also distracted. Only Gul Ragat seemed unconcerned about the atrocity they had read about. Of course, he had had several days to think about it already. *And of course, he's a Cardassian,* thought Dax bitterly.

At last, she veered away from her phaser-straight northeastern course when she saw a bluer glimmer on her right. It turned out to be a large saltwater lake.

She landed, turned to Ragat, and said, "end of the line, partner."

He startled as from a dream of long ago. "What? Here? There's nothing."

Dax bared her teeth. "Take a hike. Way back to your compound is a century and a half that-a-way." She pointed back along the course they had come. If the Gul couldn't find his way back, she decided, that was his own problem. "Keep these mountains close on your left. You'll get there."

Gul Ragat pulled a stiff upper lip, Cardassian to the end. *Must be a noble house,* she thought, understanding but unimpressed. He spoke, seemingly to no one, or to himself: "Perhaps it's for the best. I have always had my Neemak Counselor."

"What kind of counselor?"

Ragat shook his head. "Now it's a changeling. One of *those.*" He stared at her with intensity, speaking like a lost soul in an endless nightmare. "They spy on me," he explained, enunciating clearly, as if for a hidden microphone. "Now they take the form of

Cardassians and infiltrate my organization. Was Neemak a spy, do you think?"

"I don't have a clue to what you're talking about. And actually, I don't care."

Ragat smiled knowingly at Dax, smiled and winked. He bowed with slight mockery but real courtliness. "It's not important to anyone but me."

She pulled a pack from the saddlebag, twenty-eight days worth of Cardassian provisions, as demanded, lifted from the compound. "You'll pardon us if we don't wish you luck," she said. Then she started the engine, yanked the skimmer into the air, and took off, leaving the pathetic, hunched figure of a man standing by the lonely shore of the lake. He was looking, not the way they had come, the way he would return, but at the sinking sun—almost as if he saw his own life falling toward its horizon.

Then he was gone, and Dax couldn't even see him in the rear-viewer. Bashir leaned close. "You drive for a while," he said, "then it's my turn. I don't want to stop for the night. Let's put some distance between us and. . . ."

She nodded. *I know exactly what you mean, my friend.*

Kai Winn settled painfully into the overly austere chair in the Emissary's former office, behind the too-plain, too-small desk overlooked by barren walls and unornamented ceiling. The Emissary was the elect of the Prophets, but he had much to learn about the majesty of office. Perhaps he would have made a good *ranjin* or monk, but he would have served very unwell as Kai. *May the Prophets forgive me,* she appended with half her heart.

She let her head droop into her arms. There was nothing more tiring than wearing The Face, bowing and scraping to a "master" who must not under any circumstances understand how much one loathed him or that one sought any method at hand to end his plans, career, life. Winn smiled behind her arms; Nerys was surely discovering this very fact at exactly the same moment. The child, Kai Winn's secret protege (a status unknown even to the major herself), was finally beginning to grow toward adulthood: *the major is attaining majority, O joyous day.* And her secret mentor, Sister Winn, was nervously anticipating Gul Ragat's raid on the Riis spaceport, hoping that the young boy Barada Vai had understood Winn's cryptic message and warned the Resistance cell not to. . . .

No, no, that was years ago—decades! I am Kai now. Or am I still a vedek? Is Opaka still among us? No, I'm sure she is gone and I am Kai, but I'm just too weary to get up and check.

The memory-dreams were coming more frequently, striking Winn in her waking moments, not only at night. *It's because this whole adventure has turned into a waking nightmare,* she concluded. It was supposed to be so simple, so triumphant. Bajor, in the person of Kai Winn, was to assume control of the Cardassian eye that had orbited the planet for so long, watching every move of the Bajoran people. She would rename it to remove not only the stench of Cardassia but also the shame of Federation rescue when Bajor could not free itself. Once *Terok Nor*, then *Deep Space Nine*—now the station was *Emissary's Sanctuary*, a Bajoran name for a little piece of Bajor—*de facto* as well as *de jure* now.

That scheming little blasphemer Shakaar, having weaseled his way into appointment as First Minister, tried to add the title of Governor of *Emissary's Sanctuary* to his plate. But Kai Winn made sure the Council considered all its options and choices; in the end, "it was decided" that the station would be better in the hands of a proven religious leader, already so favored by the Prophets as to have been elected Kai. *"It was decided"—by me. And I must confess, I enjoyed that little exercise of authority.*

There really was nothing wrong with Shakaar. He was a good fellow, had been a loyal soldier during the Resistance. But the Prophets had had so few victories of late in the thoroughly secularized Bajoran government. It was good to win one for righteousness, for a change.

Not every popular indulgence or every move toward tolerance was good for the people—even if, childlike, they enjoyed it. A child would enjoy candy for dinner, too, and a man might enjoy intimate time spent with that poor Bajoran Dabo girl in Quark's Place. But enjoyment didn't make gluttony or adultery acceptable.

There was always duty. Duty called to everyone, from the farmer in the field to Kai in the Sky. Brothers and Sisters of faith had great duties laid upon them. Winn knew her duty; it had been writ clear from the moment the opportunity presented itself: she had to get the holocam with its precious images to the cell, to any cell. The information was so urgently needed for. . . .

There I go again, down the snakehole of old memories. Well, if the Prophets will hint so strongly, I must yield to their will.

Consciously relaxing her face, her shoulders and thoughts, Kai Winn drifted into a dark, fretful temple where she was faced with four ways to fail: if she lacked the badge of valor, she could throw the holocam into the bushes and forget all about it; if she missed the stone of wisdom, she could confide in the wrong man and be denounced; if she lost the bowl of compassion, she could condemn another, such as Barada Vai, diverting suspicion from herself. And if Winn misplaced the needle of reason. . . .

THIRTY YEARS AGO

Heavenward Prayer Spaceport, the "Palm of Bajor," was a marvel of obsolescence in an age of modernity; Sister Winn loved it beyond all its fellows. Though the Cardassians had renamed it—with typical bureaucratic inventiveness—Collection Point One, all the Bajorans still used the original name (and if the truth be told, so did nine-tenths of the Cardassians. Tradition imbued every building, floating walkway, roadway, and launch pad in the place: the passenger terminal, for example, now used for large-scale Cardassian troop transportation as well as for ferrying Cardassian notables and Bajoran untouchables to

Terok Nor, included not a single slidewalk. Instead, passengers shuffled along on foot past murals depicting the Nine Stages of the Prophet Amadan, the Beginning, the Apotheosis of Ramn, and the Gathering. That is, the Cardassian legionnaires and Bajoran prisoners walked; high-ranking Guls, legates, and other dignitaries simply "beamed" from the entry checkpoint directly to the VIP lounge, having little apparent interest in Bajoran religious artwork.

Sister Winn, crouching in a muddy ditch on the outskirts of the landing field itself, squinted against the afternoon sun, which burned her eyes even through her polarized, UV-protection, "frog-eye" sunglasses. In her discomfort, she considered the Cardassian innovation of *beaming,* disassembling a body into molecules or atoms or subatomic particles or whatever, firing it through the ether at some unholy speed, and miraculously rebuilding it at another spot, and decided that she would rather suffer an eternity of foul-smelling mud and an endless supply of mud-chiggers than ever allow herself to be atomized like the bug-spray she used in her tiny garden. *I will never, ever,* ever *voluntarily use that horrific method of transportation . . . surely it strips body from soul and leaves the latter behind.*

She pinched to death another chigger that had happily begun to gnaw on her ear. Winn had only herself to blame for her discomfort: she had led Gul Ragat to this awful vantage point, whence he could "spring his ambush" on the unsuspecting Resistance raid. *He expects to net an entire cell,* thought Sister Winn grimly, *and who's to say he won't be right?* She prayed yet again to the Prophets that the young lad,

Barada Vai, had understood her secret message and convinced the cell leaders of the lurking disaster; if prayerful repetition alone were sufficient to move the Prophets, then Winn had prayed enough to invoke Their physical presence—higher than the tallest launch tower—on the landing field itself.

CHAPTER
5

HEAVENWARD PRAYER was the forefinger of the Palm of Bajor, laid against the Kimbila Stream, the largest tributary into the Shakiristi River. It lay nearly ten Bajoran kilometers from the city of Riis proper, which itself sat at the "wrist," where the swollen Shakiristi threw itself through the final pass in the foothills of the Lakastors into the Cold Sea.

In the summer, the rolling hills would be brown, the moist hollows deepest green. Streams and rivulets collected from the Lakastor Mountains and from the sharp buttes of Granite Prayer, and chuckled down the hills, barely slowing across the valleys, until they flowed into the thundering Shakiristi.

But now it was deep, cold winter. Riis never grew cold enough to snow, but the chill wind picked at Sister Winn's bones and made her joints ache. She pulled the priestess habit tightly around her ample

flesh, wishing she had listened to her inner nag and
worn long underwear. Gul Ragat appeared impervi-
ous to the weather. He was so intent on catching his
rabbits he was practically salivating.

The spaceport itself was laid out like a gigantic
kami board: a circular causeway surrounded the
landing field, raising it above the swampy lake of
dark-green water on which the rest of Riis floated.
High ramps, reinforced now for Cardassian heavy-
tracked vehicles, drove like spokes from the "wheel"
of the causeway to the field itself at the hub. An
access road spiraled from ramp to ramp, tighter and
tighter, closing on the center of the field like a spider
web.

The buildings were arched and porticoed, colored
in muted greens and pastel pinks. They lay low,
hugging the dry elevated land. Except for the tower,
not a building rose higher than four storeys. The
controlling tower was a pyramid that thrust sky-
ward—heavenward—five times that height, domi-
nating the landscape. From the top, where a
revolving vegetarian restaurant was a customary
tourist watering hole, Sister Winn discovered she
could see all the way to Kimbilisti, forty kilometers
away. At night, the lights topping buoys on the lake
and dotting the surrounding countryside between
the Thousand Rivers of Riis looked like nothing so
much as a heaven full of stars reflected on land and
water—hence the name Heavenward Prayer.

"Where are they?" said Gul Ragat, so softly that
Winn wasn't sure whether he was talking to her or
himself.

"Your pardon, my lord?"

Ragat turned on Sister Winn the angriest face he'd ever shown her. "Where *are* they? Your little rebels . . . what are they *waiting* for?"

Winn tried to look nervous, which wasn't at all difficult. She licked her lips and discovered her tongue was just as dry. "I . . . uh . . . perhaps they're—delayed?" Her face flushed with the lie, and she hoped he would give the reaction a different interpretation.

"Perhaps," said the Gul, "they're not coming at all. Perhaps they *know* not to come."

"Give me—give them more time, my lord! They may yet come." She crouched away from the window of the inn Gul Ragat had taken over. Winn buried her face in her forearms and prayed.

Her words were a flat lie: Sister Winn already knew there was no chance whatsoever that the rebels would show up and attack the spaceport. Jaras Shie was the most punctual man in the entire Resistance—that was almost the only thing Sister Winn knew about him. If Jaras missed an attack at dawn, it could only be because he had no intention of attacking at all. Winn's prayers were not a request of the Prophets—they were words of thanksgiving.

But I do beseech the Prophets, she corrected herself. She was spared the horror of having collaborated with the Cardassians . . . but she still had a holocam full of pictures to deliver. If she failed to get the camera to Jaras's cell, then all the lives she had put at risk, including her own, would count for nothing.

"Their eyes will see every part of you," said someone from—from inside Sister Winn's own head. She looked up, sucking in a sharp inhalation. She had never "heard voices" before! For a moment, the priestess felt dizzy; a senseless fear stole across her face. *Am I going mad?* she wondered. Then, just as quickly, she understood: *Prophets, he's—they're about to search me!*

Winn stood, mouth open. Gul Ragat had never searched her, not once in the four years she had (as he thought) served him. He rarely had anyone searched, violated—never a priestess. But she knew at that moment that Ragat was going to do the unprecedented . . . and he would find the holocam. He couldn't help it . . . her trick bootheel wasn't *that* clever.

Whose voice was *that?* Flustered, she pushed her mind away from the contemplation of forbidden mysteries. Who could it have been but . . . Winn shook herself, rose, and walked with anguished stateliness to the corner farthest from the Gul and his personal bodyguards. She felt a pair of reptilian eyes tracking her movements. Turning, she beheld Counselor Neemak staring intently at a spot a little to Winn's left. *Keep watching until your eyes fall out,* she thought. *If I have nothing else, I have the patience to wait for my time.*

Winn perched herself precariously on a pile of Cardassian field packs. She folded her legs like a knotted bow, resting each hand on the opposite boot. From this position, it would be but the work of a moment to twist her right bootheel and drop the holocam into her palm—and then what?

Where in the world can I possibly hide such a suspicious object as a camera? Several minutes of thought failed to produce a plan, even a germ of one. Instead, she methodically attacked the problem from the opposite side. What, Winn asked herself, could the Cardassians find in a trick swinging heel that would *not* cause them instantly to execute her?

That's easy, she thought. *What else would an innocent Bajoran wish to conceal from prying eyes and clutchy hands but money?* She nodded, humming to herself. Wherever she found to stash the holocam, she had to replace it with a thick wad of cash in her bootheel. *Great. Now I have two miracles to pull off in place of one!*

She decided to work on the money problem first, hoping that her backbrain would continue mulling the primary puzzle of what to do with the holocam. Where, she pondered, would a Bajoran priestess get her hands *Bajoran money,* she thought; a Bajoran with a wallet full of Cardassian currency would doubtless be executed for robbery.

Once again, inspiration stepped forward and introduced itself: the only person in the Gul's entourage who would probably carry Bajoran bills was the half-Bajoran, half-Cardassian Neemak Counselor, who made a career of playing both sides against the middle and pocketing the squeeze. A brief smile flickered across Sister Winn's face, almost too quick even for her to catch it. Neemak had already lost interest in her, his own patience long since exhausted.

It was time, decided the holy one, to put to good use some of the tricks a lonely, friendless seminary student had practiced while her fellow students were laughing and socializing and ignoring her. *It's been a long time since I slickered anyone's pocket . . . if the Prophets love me as I love Them, let Them guide my hands now.*

"Winn!" shouted Gul Ragat.

"Yes, lord?" said Winn, jumping to her feet.

"Come here. Now."

Winn never waited to be told twice. She rushed to the side of her Gul, who still stared out the window at the controlling tower, a quarter-kilometer from the inn. "I am here, M'lord Ragat, to be commanded."

He turned to face her, looking for the first time like a real Cardassian. His jaw clenched like Legate Migar's. His trapezius muscles, absurdly prominent as on any Cardassian, were as rigid and hard as Gul Dukat's. His fist clenched like Colonel Akkat's had just before he had struck Winn in the face at the bulletin tea, four days and a thousand years ago. Ragat had intervened on Winn's behalf then; now he looked as though he would cheer her hanging.

"Barada Vai," whispered the Gul, as if not trusting his voice not to break. Winn said nothing, wearing the mask of serenity she had long ago developed; a professional face—expectant, calm, but slightly puzzled. "Your *brother*. You do remember your brother, don't you?"

"Yes, of course, m'lord. What about Vai? He's just a child."

An evil presence loomed behind her. Without turning, Sister Winn knew the breath of Neemak. But Ragat seemed not to notice.

"Even a child has a mouth," said the Gul, words winding about her neck like a squeeze-snake. "So I begin to think."

"Oh, no, surely not, most gracious lord!"

"But he *could have* talked," said Ragat in a perfectly horrid, quiet voice; "couldn't he have? If, that is, he somehow guessed that we planned a raid. What a lucky guess!"

Neemak, irresistibly drawn by secrets and whispers, began to edge toward the pair, surely stretching both his ears. Winn carefully kept her eyes exclusively on Ragat, though she itched to see how close Neemak was going to get—and to begin a visual search for where the counselor kept his ill-gotten bribe-money. *Best not to give the Gul any excuse to find me insubordinate.*

Ragat turned his back on Winn, but she knew she still had his full attention, even as he stared at the sleepy, unexploded controlling tower—as untouched, as unattacked as it had been yesterday and would be tomorrow. It was the symbol of his humiliation, and possibly his ruin, if Neemak were but to put two threes together and get six. After a moment, Sister Winn bowed deeply, backing away with humility.

And with half-lidded eyes expertly scanning the half-man to her left. Neemak did not notice; he was too busy trying to penetrate Gul Ragat's open-faced frustration. Winn was suddenly surprised to feel talents she had long since renounced flooding back through her brain and hands. She had immediately seen the pocket that bulged beneath Neemak's black, leather overcoat. . . .

It had been a long time ago, back in the seminary. Winn was not the most well-liked religious student. In fact, she was held in disdain by the fashionably agnostic crowd. When she'd fallen sick with a nerve disorder, a few visited her dorm room out of a sense of duty, but nobody came in friendship.

So Winn, in a perverse moment of her life (never since repeated), studied and practiced the simple art of removing a wallet from a pocket . . . more to restore manual dexterity than for any criminological reasons. After several months of illness, Winn got quite expert at the obsolete talent . . . enough so that she could play a few practical jokes on her "friends," slipping valuables into a pocket that would fall out when the mark reached for his handkerchief.

She knew she was good. But never before had she found occasion to slicker a pocket for real. It provoked a heavy feeling of stage fright, now that she was lightening the pockets of the counselor—evil incarnate.

Neemak was no soldier, but he always wore his greatcoat unbuttoned for quick access to the pistol he kept in a back-draw holster. He was distracted. There was no better moment . . . certainly none before it would be too late for the priestess, so her inner certainty told her.

Before Winn could think twice and perhaps talk herself out of it, she stretched out her hand as she continued to back past Neemak Counselor. Her left hand caught the edge of the thick, stiff greatcoat, drawing it back. She stepped behind him, placing her right hand near his right hip pocket, finger-ends lightly touching the billfold. *Now all I need is a distraction,* she thought . . . prayed.

"Barada Vai," said Ragat, definitely to himself this time. "Barada damned Vai!"

"Barada Vai, M'Lord Gul?" repeated Neemak, probing.

The reaction from Ragat took Winn's breath away. Never a granite-face, never one to wear the mask, the Gul whirled to face his counselor-spy with an expression of guilty astonishment, a thief caught with his hand actually inside the lockbox. His face drained, and his mouth opened and closed. *Prophets above,* thought Winn, *he had no idea the silent-footed Neemak was skulking behind him. No clue whatsoever!*

And Neemak, no fool in the wiles of intrigue, knew he had struck a vein of purest ore: guilty secrets were lifeblood to Neemak. He smiled, stepping forward eagerly to confront Ragat inside his personal space with the terrible secret he had just learned. Winn stepped quickly, so he wouldn't feel a tug on his greatcoat. "Barada Vai," said Neemak, calculating, "the child you spoke to in the square. Where you waited . . . as if waiting for Barada himself."

Ragat said nothing, but he slowly shook his head.

"As we wait here now! How many times, m'lord, have you glanced out that window at the tower? As if you were . . . *waiting* for something to happen."

Gul Ragat giggled like a schoolgirl. Neemak brought his hands together as if washing them. And holy Sister Winn clipped the folded bills between forefinger and middle finger and slickered them as smoothly as a carny. Heart pounding, she slowly let the greatcoat close again, then stepped back farther into the opposite corner, sitting once more on the teetering pile of Cardassian field packs.

The voices of Gul and counselor dropped to a whisper, and both glanced back at Sister Winn. She waited until Ragat began to sweat. He backed away from Neemak to restore his space, and the counselor stepped forward, "chasing" the Gul in slow motion around the room. *How familiar that is,* thought Winn to herself, smiling. She had been in Gul Ragat's very situation at a seminar once, slowly pursued by vedek Dasa, intent upon making some obscure philosophical point, until she was rescued by vedek Opaka and vedek Marinasa.

The Cardassian-and-a-half had completely forgotten she was even there, so intent were they upon the dance of spider and fly. She fanned the bills . . . *too much, far too much.* No Bajoran would have as much money as Neemak carried. She quickly discarded all the biggest bills (and all the Cardassian money) into her palm, keeping only as much as a thrifty priestess might have saved over a few years.

She glanced again at the pair of intriguers. Then she swallowed a lump of dust, crossed her legs again, and twisted her heel open. The holocam tumbled out, and she caught it, barely preventing it from thumping on the floor. Fumbling the bills into the secret compartment, all her dexterity suddenly vanished. She swung the heel closed again and breathed a sigh of relief.

But a moment later, her heart jumped as she realized that now she held *a camera full of classified holos* in her hand, a hand that shook with palsy. She stared around the hotel room, desperate for another inspiration from the Prophets—anything!—telling her what to do next.

Dresser. Liquor cabinet. Wardrobe. Wash basin. Sink. A bed for the rugged Gul while his legionnaires camped in the old grazing field. A comm screen, a writing desk. Her eyes were drawn back to the wardrobe, then to Gul Ragat's own field pack. *Why, by the Prophets, does he carry that, when he sleeps in a luxurious spaceport hotel? He never even unpacks it.*

The words rustled through Winn's head like dried leaves along a concrete walk: *He never even unpacks it!*

Thought became deed in the wink of an eye. She rose, crossed to the walk-in closet, and dropped the holocam into a side pocket of the field pack. After a moment's thought, she gently pressed the pocket-flap closed, where the fuzzy-hooks held it shut. Then, hearing the discussion slowing, she sat in the nearest seat, a hard, cold, "proper Cardassian chair." She sat at attention and once again put on the mask.

Minutes later, as a grim-faced Gul led them out of the hotel room and into his household's camp in the grassy field that once had been a grazing pasture, she found no difficulty casting away the excess currency that she was still palming, the large denominations and all the Cardassian bills, even with Neemak Counselor breathing down her neck like a wild beast. It never occurred to him that anyone would throw away money, and he did not notice what he could not see. *Let the wind hide my deed,* thought Sister Winn.

Gul Ragat waited, quietly fuming, in the hotel lobby, accompanied by his increasingly worried personal priestess and his gloating counselor. The sun crawled across the sky, then began to walk, and finally sprinted through the last few hours. Sister Winn sat on a couch watching Cardassian news bulletins—nothing interesting, but she wasn't paying attention anyway—until she looked up and it was night. There was no attack; Heavenward Prayer Spaceport bustled as it always did, shouting with its usual cacophony, stuffed as full as ever with Bajorans and Cardassians from here to there and back to here. A moment later, Winn found herself with the unwanted but undivided attention of three Cardassian legionnaires and her own personal Gul.

"Yes, my—my lord?" She allowed a note of fear and uncertainty to color her words.

"I never thought it would be you," said Ragat.

"Me?" Winn's voice sounded tiny and childlike, even to her own ears, and she didn't need to fake it.

"To betray me!" Gul Ragat's face grew stony and gray, and he spoke through a jaw clenched tight. Winn saw every muscle in the young Gul's body flexed. Behind his Cardassian eyes, she saw obsidian.

"I? Betray your grace? Prophets forbid I should ever betray anyone to whom I owe my loyalty!" Winn squirmed off the couch and fell to her knees, prostrating herself before the furious Gul. "Please, I beg you—do not blame me, m'lord! I don't know what happened, why they didn't . . ." She let her voice trail away. Looking up, she stared between Gul Ragat and Neemak Counselor, between rage mingled with its own fear and a triumphant smirk shaken with a drop of nervous confusion: Neemak knew that he knew something, but he didn't yet know *what* he knew.

But Gul Ragat, like Sister Winn, would know that once the half-breed got his *yarpi*-teeth into a dirty secret, he wouldn't let go until he had swallowed every drop. And Ragat knew it might ultimately prove his ruin . . . he had withheld information, and by his negligence (and his trusting of a Bajoran) missed the opportunity to capture one of the most effective cells of the Resistance. Cardassia Prime was not forgiving of stupidity.

He mouthed a single word silently at her: *Barada,* it was. Winn said nothing; what else could the Gul think? *He doesn't even know how right he is,* she thought with little satisfaction.

"Take her," he said abruptly. "And if she resists or attempts to escape—kill her." Winn sighed, sitting back on her rump. She could see that the words tasted bitter to Ragat . . . yet still, he had forced them out. *Congratulations,* she thought, *you have just ordered your first murder. You are now a full-fledged Cardassian.*

She rose quickly and went with the sergeant and the two private legionnaires, giving them no excuse whatsoever to carry out the Gul's conditional order, for some Cardassians were only too eager for red-work. She paused only long enough to look back at the young man, barely even twenty-one, and to allow a single tear to roll down her cheek. "M'lord," she said, "I thought you knew me better." Then the unsentimental soldiers yanked her toward the revolving doors and hustled her faster than she cared to walk toward the encampment.

Winn stumbled twice on the cobblestones between the lobby door and the grassy pasture. As she was shoved through the camp, the Bajorans who had relied upon her for so much of their spiritual needs, their hope, their lives as anything but slaves, turned their faces away and pretended not to notice. They gave her no support. One young Bajoran boy yelled a rude rhyme at her implying she was a woman of small virtue, but a woman cuffed him and he shut up.

They reached the tent that would be her designated prison. As the sergeant yanked open the tent flap, a Cardassian was blocking their way. With a gasp, Winn realized it was the same sadistic guard who had seen her drop off the edge of Surface 92. The corporal's own mouth fell open in shock . . . Winn was the Gul's favorite! How could *she* be in such trouble? But then he recovered. He spread his feet, hooked thumbs in his belt, and began to bray. "Well, well, well! Look what we have here! So it looks like I wuz right after all that, and you're a traitor just like I—"

Without pausing or missing a step, the sergeant grabbed the bullying corporal by his breastplate and jerked him out of the way and onto his posterior. The sergeant shoved Sister Winn into the tent without a backward glance. The corporal sputtered and leapt to his feet, shouting slurs in Cardassian against the sergeant's manhood and loyalty, words that

Winn barely knew—and would never admit to knowing.

Only then did the sergeant turn. He stared silently at the bully, saying nothing, just looking. The corporal's voice faltered, then he struggled to silence. Without a word, the sergeant grimly drew his thumb across his own throat in a gesture as universal as it was chilling.

The corporal grew distinctly ashen, confirming what Winn had long thought about such sadistic thugs. Then, with a sick smile, he backed slowly away. Sister Winn prayed she would never see him again . . . but fretted that she would.

The sergeant turned back to her. "Search her," he said without emotion. "Strip her clothes, her boots, her bag, and catalog everything. Then we will prepare for the interrogation."

Winn offered no resistance. She had the patience to wait for her time.

CHAPTER
6

KIRA THE SLAVE watched quietly for her chance. From Kai Winn she was starting to learn the patience to wait for her time. At last, three days following the last "prisoner" roundup, the dean ordered her to the Promenade to talk to Garak: the aliens had decided that all the captives should wear uniform clothing, and they chose the tailor, naturally enough, to design and replicate it.

It was a strange feeling for Kira, being so anxious to speak to a Cardassian—and in particular, *this* Cardassian. But Garak had been in the Obsidian Order, and much as he still turned Kira's stomach, she needed that expertise.

"There is something completely wrong about the way they're acting," she whispered to Garak, in between conveying the dean's uniform-design instructions. She looked around nervously: with Kai

Winn's inexplicable help, the aliens had reprogrammed the computer to eavesdrop on their captives throughout the station using hidden audio pickups.

Garak instantly put his finger to his lips. He went around his shop, starting several cloth-cutting and - attaching machines. Then he touched his ear and drew his finger across his throat. Kira interpreted Garak's signal as telling her the noise from the machines would interfere with the computer's ability to eavesdrop . . . *in fact,* thought Kira, *I'll bet he designed them that way deliberately. A Cardassian, especially* this *Cardassian, trusts no one.*

But that was the very expertise she needed. "Which peculiarities have you noticed?" asked Garak, with the faint, I-know-more-than-you smile Kira despised more than anything else about him.

"Well, they refer to us as prisoners—"

"We are."

"Instead of captives or hostages," she finished, glaring at Garak. "And then there's the episode with the civilians in the bombardment shelters." Garak raised his brows questioningly, and Kira explained what had happened. Meanwhile, the Cardassian worked on a sketch of the proposed uniforms, and he and Kira pointed to various sections and reworked them, in case the aliens had installed spy-eyes as well.

"I would think they were soldiers," said Kira, "or even police officers. Except for what they call themselves."

"Yes, few police renegades would call themselves 'the Liberated.'"

Kira gave Garak a hard look, but she didn't bother asking how he had come by his knowledge. He would never tell her anyway. After a moment, Garak continued. "But our quasi-cops certainly appear to be driving police-style ships."

Kira blinked. "They are?"

"Well they're certainly not military vessels, or you would have them in your security database. Oh, I *do* beg your pardon," said Garak, bowing. "I should not have implied that I have access to your security database. I was only extrapolating from the fact that your do not seem to recognize the ships, yet I'm sure you consulted the database the moment they attacked the station."

The major fumed. It was obvious that Garak did, in point of fact, mean to imply exactly that . . . but did that mean he had or hadn't broken into the top-security Starfleet intelligence database? Was he just playing games, or did he really know?

"They didn't have the kind of weaponry that has been used against us before," she said, thinking out loud, "these, what did you call them? Quasi-cops."

"Or there would be little left of *Terok*—my apologies, of *Emissary's Sanctuary*. But tell me, Major Kira. . . ." Garak hunched closer on the pretext of redrawing a section of the sleeve. "Why didn't you use those wonderful quantum torpedoes of yours, those that your Captain Sisko used so effectively in the recent unpleasantness involving Cardassia?" He smiled without guile, by which Kira knew he was full of it.

"There were technical difficulties." *I'll be damned if I'll tell him anything,* she promised herself.

"It's almost as if . . . as if you didn't have the *authorization* to fire them. Or some such problem. Why, can you be telling me that the vaunted Federation doesn't trust you with the access codes? Tsk, tsk." He shook his head sadly. "They're getting more devious and suspicious with every passing day. I daresay, the Federation is almost starting to get *Cardassian* on us."

Kira curled her lip, feeling an overwhelming urge to slam her fist into his Carassian face. But she knew any violent impulse would be detected by the slave collar she wore—in fact, it was already beginning to tighten. *Ten bars of latinum says the bastard knows all about the collar, too.*

It was a bet she quickly won. "Well," said Garak, "at least I ought to be able to help you with that." His eyes flickered briefly to the torc, pressing into Kira's flesh.

"Can you—deactivate?" she said, gasping for a thin, reedy breath.

The Cardassian nodded, smiling and studying the uniform design. "A small piece, a sliver in the right place, can short out the entire mechanism. We've used similar devices ourselves. I'll work on it and slip it to you when it's ready."

She controlled her breath, calming herself. There was no alternative to working with Garak the Spy. "So we have police cruisers driven by quasi-cop aliens who call themselves the Liberated. And they're desperate for an Orb—don't tell me you didn't already know that."

"Major!" Garak looked scandalized.

76

"But *why?* What the hell do they want with it? Why would any non-Bajoran race want to speak to the Prophets?"

The instant the words were out of her mouth, Kira gasped, not even remembering to hide the reaction from any lurking spy-cams. Garak smiled; the thought had already occurred to him, she was sure, but now she knew as well . . . and no need to risk being overheard by saying it aloud.

Why would any race want to speak to the Prophets, the "wormhole aliens," as the captain used to call them before he became Emissary? Because the Prophets were a dangerous unknown. Kira didn't think it possible that the Prophets could be turned away from Bajor, but another race might not know that. Even the thought that the Prophets might abandon Bajor was blasphemous. *But blasphemies have come to pass before,* she thought cynically. That the aliens might succeed in subverting or perhaps even *harming* the Prophets was a chance she could not take.

Somehow, she had to warn Kai Winn. It was vital, desperately vital, that the alien dean *not* get his hands on an Orb under any circumstances. The fate not only of Bajor but of the entire Alpha Quadrant hung in the balance.

But the Kai was surrounded and constantly watched by the aliens, as if they knew, like Kira, that Kai Winn was the key. Since the moment of the Kai's surrender of the station, the aliens had not allowed the two women to be alone together for a single moment. *And how,* wondered Kira, thinking of a Cardassian game of strategy she had studied as a young soldier, *how to pass through a fortress of stone to whisper the word in the ear of the queen?*

But she wasn't to get the chance. Garak's door slid open without a preceding chirp, and two of the quasi-cops strode into the tailor's shop. "May I help you, gentlemen?" asked the Cardassian. "Have you come about the uniforms? I have the preliminary designs right here. I've been working hard on them."

Kira admired his smoothness. Her own heart was pounding in excitement. The bugs ignored Garak and walked straight to the major. "You will come," said one of them. "The dean requires your presence in the cell-block control center."

"And where is the cell-block control center?" But the aliens did not answer, each taking one of Kira's arms and hustling her toward the door.

They dragged her to the turbolift, entered, and said nothing. The lift moved on its own—up to Ops. The Kai, the dean, and several other Bajorans and aliens were arrayed in a parabola, waiting for her.

The moment she entered, the dean made a flat statement that he meant as a question: "You work with members of the military unit called Starfleet." Kira uncomfortably noticed she was at the focus of the parabola.

After a slow, shuffling moment, during which she pretended to have difficulty understanding the question (she had quickly relearned the traditional Bajoran game played against occupying forces), she nodded. "Yes, sir. I know some people in Starfleet."

"Please observe the forward surveillance monitor," said the dean. Kira obediently turned and felt her stomach roll silently. Sitting dead in space relative to the station, but inverted, since it had its own gravity of course, was a Galaxy-class Federation starship, the *U.S.S. Harriman.* It was sending a hailing message to the current "owners" of *Emissary's Sanctuary* . . . considering that possession, Kira remembered reading somewhere, was nine-tenths of the law.

"This is Admiral Taggart, captain of the Federation starship *Harriman,* speaking to the Dominion force currently holding *Deep Space Nine.* We have received a plea from a former ranking officer of this station—" Kira winced, feeling the Kai's glare of betrayal burning the back of her neck—"that you be removed from the premises immediately. You have ten minutes to commence evacuation, or we declare an act of war and initiate counterforce to recover our possession."

Major Kira shrank within her uniform at the words, as ill-chosen as they possibly could have been. Not only at the arrogance of this Admiral Taggart, proclaiming that *Emissary's Sanctuary* was a "possession" of the Federation, but even more at his extraordinary inability to predict the most obvious response from a group of terrorists holding hostages on an occupied military base. *What the hell does he* think *they're going to do?*

Kira heard no order to open a channel, but the dean began to speak a response. "I am dean of the Liberated. You have ten minutes by your time to depart from the range of these scanning instruments. If you do not depart, we will execute one prisoner every five minutes. To show our resolve, we shall execute two prisoners immediately."

Kira said nothing, her throat constricting so tight, she probably couldn't have spoken if she'd wanted. Kai Winn was likewise silent. Both leaders had been through such "displays" before . . . during the last occupation of Bajoran territory. They knew the drill. It was the hardest thing Kira had ever had to do in all her years in the Resistance: to stand still and watch friends and battlefield comrades murdered rather than yield and betray the rest.

But she almost lost her fragile grip when the dean issued the command to his troops. "Take two female prisoners from cell-block Shelter Seven to the transporter chamber, execute them, and transport their bodies to the bridge of the vessel *Harriman*."

"The problem with Cardassian skimmers," said Dax, shouting over Bashir's shoulder against a horrific wind, "is that they're Cardassian."

The doctor said nothing, but he thought a few words and phrases he was too much a gentleman ever to say aloud, even to a centuries-old Trill. Speech was an annoyance: Bashir was too busy cranking and straining against the controls of the two-man cycle-like skimmer that had suddenly, two hours before, grown a mind of its own. It had wrenched itself off course and veered sharply to the right.

"Julian! Get this thing under control!"

"Perhaps *you'd* like to try it," he snapped. Notwithstanding what could have been considered an offer, Bashir continued tugging on the handlebars for the simple reason that he happened to be sitting in front. "What is this blasted thing *doing?*"

"Julian, I think somebody whistled and it's going home." Dax sounded worried.

"Um . . . Gul Ragat?"

"Are you kidding? That old man can't be more than ten kilometers from where we left him, fifteen if he's highly motivated. And he doesn't have a communicator—I searched him myself." She was quiet a moment, then drew the same conclusion that Bashir had already drawn. "It must be a general recall . . . something has happened, and the Cardassians are retreating to regroup."

Bashir pursed his lips. The obvious conclusion to leap to was that the "something" was Benjamin Sisko. But he hardly needed to suggest the possibility to Jadzia Dax, the captain's "old man."

The doctor stopped trying to physically wrench it back on their previous course and settled back, panting. "Commander, if this skimmer is heading home, then it's heading . . ."

"Straight into the arms of a Cardassian expeditionary force," she said, her voice barely audible against the whistle of the wind and the whine of a siren that had started up when the skimmer made a sharp right turn. "Julian," she said, leaning over the side and staring downward, "how high would you estimate we are?"

"I'm not a pilot, Jadzia. But I'd say—fifty meters?"

"What would happen if we—"

"Splattered across the desert like a pair of broken eggs." He sighed, staring at the console before him: the touchplates and buttons were all completely dead; he had already tried them. Whatever broadcast command had turned the sled, it had taken complete control.

Dax was still leaning over, but now she started monkeying with the engine. "I wonder," she said. "Julian, do you have something long and thin, like a—like a . . ."

"Probe?"

"Yes, that's perfect. Hand it over, Doc."

Balancing on the wobbly skimmer, Bashir fished in his medical pouch, extracting his oldest and least delicate plastic probe, ordinarily used to separate tissue from a wound for visual inspection. He handed it to the commander, who began poking at the high-speed, high-power turbine assembly. "Um, Commander . . . if you jam a probe in those blades, assuming it doesn't yank your hand off, wouldn't it just—"

With a Klingon war cry, Dax thrust the probe as if stabbing a *d'k tahg* knife into an enemy's innards. The scream of metal almost burst the doctor's eardrums, and the skimmer commenced bucking and sashaying. He wrapped both arms around the handlebars, and Dax grabbed his slim waist in a death-lock that forced all the air out of his lungs.

The skimmer began to fly apart in mid-air. Shards of metal were ejected at high velocity, one of them slashing through Bashir's pants-leg and razoring his shin with a horribly painful cut to the bone. But he had neither time nor breath to shout, for as the skragged engine dropped from the frame the skimmer assumed the aerodynamic characteristics of a brick.

On the plus side, he regained control of the now-nearly-useless flight surfaces. The skimmer fluttered in a flat spin. There was one chance . . . if the spin acted like the blades of the ancient *helicopter,* which Bashir had flown in one of his spy-simulations with Garak, it might slow their fall enough for them to survive.

The spin increased. Rather than fight it, he did everything he could to encourage it. After a moment, he realized he was dangling from the handlebars, near the axis of rotation, as if gravity were now directly behind them. He clenched his teeth against the acceleration, straining his abdominal muscles to keep the blood in his head from rushing to his feet. *If I black out,* he thought dizzily, *I let go and we both die.*

But straining made little difference. They were experiencing probably five Gs of acceleration, and without the anti-G suits worn by pilots back in the twentieth century, they hadn't a hope. Bashir felt Dax's arms suddenly go limp and knew she had just lost consciousness. He caught her with his legs, but he couldn't hold on long. If only they would hit the ground; then it would all be over, one way or another. *Goodbye, cruel world,* he thought—*my last stupid joke.*

He felt something start to slip from his side—*my medical bag!* Letting go the handlebar with one hand, he grabbed the bag just as it was torn from his shoulder. Instead, he felt his other pouch—full of useful survival equipment—fly away to be lost in the desert sands. But he knew his priorities: the principle of triage worked in many surprising places.

But the single hand with which he held on was not strong enough for both his own and Dax's weight. The post was wrenched out of his hand. Dax disappeared; he couldn't even remember when she slipped out of his leg clamp. The world was a black-and-gray swirl, and Bashir's head spun so he had no clue as to which way was down.

Somebody punched him hard in the stomach, cracking two ribs and leaving him gasping and struggling for oxygen. He couldn't see, couldn't even tell whether his eyes were open or closed . . . but luminous blackness filled his "vision," or his visual cortex, at least. *Oh God, here comes the headache,* he just had time to think before the pain struck. It was so intense, it forced an involuntary grunt out of him, and he knew he was alive and on the deck.

Nausea overwhelmed Bashir, and he lost every undigested scrap he had eaten in the past twelve hours. When he finished, he blinked his eyes open. They were blurry, but his normal visual acuity soon returned. Shaking, tears and mucous dripping down his face, Bashir rose to his knees and looked for Dax.

She was lying on her side about a hundred meters from his position. He tried to move, but the pain in his chest stabbed him, and he inhaled raggedly. *Punctured lung,* he realized. Gallantry told him to ignore it and walk, crawl, whatever it took to get to Dax's side. But the intelligence that had often frightened him as a child (after his "treatment") began to speak inside his head in calm, emotionless tones:

you'll be a lot better help to her, it said, if you're in good health yourself. Repair your own injuries first.

He hated the voice of reason, but as usual, he could find no fault with it. "Have you," he gasped to himself, "ever tried—to fix—your own broken— ribs and punctured—lung?" The answer was no, but Bashir discovered to his surprise that it was possible . . . assuming one were as flexible as a monkey. He played the tissue restorer across his chest a dozen times before his breathing settled; it took longer to knit the bones, but he was finished with everything in less than three minutes.

He pushed to his feet, ignoring the remaining tenderness, and stumbled across the pebbly sand to Dax. Trill luck had worked as advertised: Dax had fallen first, when they were still too high, but she had landed in a soft sandpit. She was unconscious but still breathing, rasping so loud that Bashir decided she had a fractured skull even before he used the medical tricorder. The skull fracture wasn't serious, but she had a compound fracture of her radius that required immediate treatment before she bled to death (and she already had a head start).

After fifteen minutes of very basic emergency medicine, the commander moaned and shifted to a less uncomfortable position. Her eyes opened. She looked at the torn, bloody sleeve of her native costume, then at the exposed arm with the characteristic pink splotch of regenerated tissue. "Miracles of mod—modern medicine," she said, mumbled actually. Then she fell into a deep sleep . . . partly due to fatigue, partly the mild sedative Bashir had hyposprayed into her shoulder.

He allowed her to sleep for two hours while he scavanged everything useful from the wreckage of the skimmer. He clawed his way into the onboard computer brain and found the transponder, smashing it to rubble so the Cardassians couldn't use it to locate the crash site. Then he returned to Dax, squatting over her.

"You look so peaceful when you sleep," he said. "I toss and moan like a patient with a fever." Bashir sighed. Then, setting practical judgment above medical wisdom, he gently shook her awake.

Dax sat bolt upright, gasping in terror, eyes like saucers. She gripped his wrists painfully hard, staring past him at the lengthening shadows of the desert of Sierra-Bravo. Then she blinked, coming fully awake. "What—what—what a nightmare," she said, shuddering.

"Nightmare? Don't Trills thrash around when they dream?"

Dax shook her head, clearing cobwebs, not responding to the question. "All right, Julian. Now what?"

"At least we're not headed for the last roundup with the Cardassian cowboys."

She lowered her brows, studying him. "You say very strange things sometimes. How much time do you spend in Quark's holosuites, anyway?"

Bashire smiled at the old Dax. "I'm a student of history. Come, let's start walking and find some shelter for the night. From the sand dunes, I'd guess we might get some wind when the sun sets."

They charted a course for the nearest range of hills. But before they could reach them, the breeze kicked up, as Bashir had prophesied. Soon the sand was blasting their faces, stinging like a swarm of angry bees. Through the painful, dangerous sandstorm, Bashir thought he saw a faint luminescence in the distance.

"Lights!" he shouted. "Maybe it's a Native village!"

"Where? I don't see anything."

"Trust me, it's there," he said. *The curse of seeing twenty-fifteen,* he thought; *nobody ever believes you.* As they got closer, the light increased until even Dax could see it. Soon, Bashir could see clumps of houses and other buildings looming in the blackness, and they cut close to minimize the sand damage to their exposed flesh. But none of the buildings were lit, and they all looked deserted. The light he had seen from two kilometers distant was a tiny, starlight lightglobe at the top of a striped pole in the center of town. A hexagon of pavement surrounded the pole. *Probably a bandstand of some sort,* he decided.

Near the bandstand was a garage-like building whose doors were not locked. Dax helped him wrestle the sliding door up—there was probably a button that would have raised it automatically, but they hadn't time to hunt for it. They ducked inside and began to shake out the sand. The doctor fished some facial cream from his MediKit, and he and Dax repaired the sand lacerations.

"Do you have a light?" he asked. "I lost everything but the medical gear back on the skimmer."

Dax fumbled in her jacket, checking all the internal pockets. "Damn," she said; "my hand torch is gone. Wait, I have something." From what Bashir could see in the starlight that filtered through a window in the ceiling, it was a tube a quarter-meter long, two centimeters in diameter.

Dax took it in both hands and made as if she was trying to break it. Bashir heard a pop, and a faint green glowing mess swirled in the center of the tube. Dax shook it violently, and the entire tube glowed brilliant green, lighting the room.

"One of Quark's," she said, smiling. "I filtched it from him during the first away-team mission." She held the glowtube aloft and gasped. "Oh, my," she said breathlessly.

"What is it?" Bashir turned to look. He saw some peculiar object hulking in the deep shadows at the back of the building.

"Oh, my!"

"Dax, what is it?" He began to see the outlines of a large, rectangular compartment with seats, storage areas, and a pair of controls that looked like hospital exercise bars hooking over the front seats and dangling down about hand height.

Bashir's mouth fell open. "Dax, it's . . ."

"Julian, it's a—"

The Native aircar taunted them with its nearness. Even if they had fathomed its inner workings, there was no way they could take off and fly in the dark in such a storm. "Sleep well," said Bashir, more to the aircar than his companion. "I have a feeling it's back to basic pilot training in the morning."

CHAPTER 7

JADZIA DAX forced herself to lie down, she even closed her eyes, but she positively refused to listen to her inner worm and sleep. She lay more or less immobile for the five hours until morning, not wanting to wake Bashir (assuming the good doctor wasn't likewise feigning sleep to avoid bothering *her*). But the moment the sun cast its first tentative rays through the still swirling dust, a natural searchlight illuminating the curious Native car, she was up and inspecting the bizarre piece of equipment.

Bashir was at her side in an instant. "So you *were* faking it," she said.

"Sleep?" said he. "What's that? I don't believe I've had a wink since we bubbled up from the *Defiant*."

"Let's see," said Dax, ticking off her fingers. "We

fought a sea monster, were ejected from a destroyed runabout, swallowed half the ocean—"

"Well, you did, at any rate."

"Stole a pair of skimmers and dumped one, took out an entire Cardassian strike team, kidnapped a Gul and dropped him in the middle of nowhere, crashed the *other* skimmer. . . ."

"And found out where the Natives came from," said a quiet Bashir. Dax trailed into silence, abruptly uninterested in her own witty repartee. Remembering the ghastly experiment in which ninety million Native children had been allowed to die, just to see whether civilization would spring magically from technology, had sobered her mood.

"Commander," said the doctor, "are we ready to get this—air-buggy moving?" Dax nodded, leading the way to the vehicle that was slowly becoming visible in the dawn light.

The passenger compartment was enclosed by a roll-cage, but the seats were bare blue metal—the "exercise-bar" steering linkages were slightly stiff to Dax's touch. *Any looser and they'd be impossible to hold steady,* she realized.

There was no obvious engine. Storage boxes— trunks—occupied the entire space behind the seats. Other than the linkages, the boxes, and the seats, the rest of the air-buggy was empty space enclosed by bars. The contraption sat on landing skids instead of wheels; it clearly was intended never to move along the ground.

"Maybe we'd better climb inside, Jadzia," said the doctor. Dax was dubious about the missing engine, but there was nothing else to do except set her eyes on the horizon and start marching.

"I *really* don't want to walk a few hundred kilometers," she said, provoking a puzzled glance from Bashir.

She clambered inside, ducking her way through the cage bars and squirming into a seat that was just slightly disproportionate to the Trill frame. "So how do you make it go?" she asked; "or how would you make it go if there were an engine?" Experimentally, she took hold of the overhead crane-like steering link with both hands and pushed forward.

The air-buggy leapt up a meter in altitude, then lurched forward like a runabout on maximum thrusters, hurling Dax back in her seat with bone-cracking acceleration. With a horrible, metal-on-metal, wrenching sound that tore at Dax's ears, the buggy shattered the back of the garage, shredding bits of steel like tissue paper. Panicked, she let go of the link, and the air-buggy slowed to a stop. But it didn't settle back on the ground; it remained a long step in the air. There was no sound of turbine or fan or even the hum of Federation-style antigravity units. Whatever science held the buggy aloft, it was silent as the grave.

"Jadzia! Are you all right?"

Dax didn't answer. She was too busy scanning three hundred and sixty degrees around them, looking for an energy signature.

"Commander? Did you find something?"

"Julian, this car isn't running on broadcast power."

"Is there an internal power source? I thought you said there was no engine or energy-storage cell. If it's not broadcast, then what?"

"I said it wasn't broadcast *power*. Julian . . ." Dax looked up, silently analyzing the bizarre and contradictory tricorder readings. "Julian, it's running on broadcast *potentia*, not power. An uncollapsed state vector that is sent around the planet instantaneously, at infinite speed. Because it's not real, it's not bound by special relativity."

"Broadcast *potential* energy? That's the most unheard-of thing I ever heard of." She barely remembered reading about broadcast potentia herself, and that was in a speculative engineering-fiction magazine, long ago.

"Well, the buggy must convert the potentia into actual power somehow. Then it just—moves. In any case," she said, feeling practical, "we've got our wheels—well, so to speak."

Bashir tried out the linkage, pushing it ever so slightly. His more-than-humanly delicate touch allowed the car to accelerate slowly. Twisting the linkage left or right steered the buggy, and pulling back stopped it, or reversed it if it were already stopped. *The simplest possible control,* thought Dax.

"And where does Madam wish to go?" asked Bashir, trying to sound like a butler in a old English holoplay.

She smiled. "Believe it or not, I had time to analyze the path that Cardassian skimmer followed when it was summoned. *If* we're right that the Cardassians are regrouping—and that Benjamin is the cause—then I think I know where he must be, judging from the Cardies' position."

"I don't understand how you get from A to B to D," said Bashir, sounding almost petulant. "Whatever happened to C, the relative position of the captain and the Cardassians?"

"Look," said Dax, holding her hands like a fighter jock describing a low-level, impulse-engine dogfight, "if Ben's here, then the Cardassians would be here; so if they're *here,* then he must be there!"

Bashir sighed and pondered the information. He didn't seem entirely to believe it. *Well,* thought Dax, *he's right;* half of her "analysis" was really a wild-eyed guess. But three-hundred-year-old intuition was not to be dismissed out of hand. "All right," he said, frowning dubiously. "Ah, *lead* on, MacDuff." The doctor winked at her.

"Julian, there's hope for you yet." She showed Bashir the course, and he set off across the plain, the air-buggy rising and falling to keep a steady altitude of one meter-plus off the deck.

The Natives advanced behind the column of away-team members. *Sure, they're called Vanimastavvi now,* thought Chief O'Brien, stepping nimbly, despite his bulk, over fallen logs, goopy quicksand, and ducking low branches. It was damnably hard keeping track of all the names Colonel-Mayor Asta-ha concocted every few days. Annoyed, O'Brien decided to stick with Natives, the most descriptive name.

He followed Commander Worf, who followed

Odo, who flapped on ahead as a local hawk, as he had before when scouting Cardassians. But the chief kept his eyes on the captain, looking for a special command.

Finally, after nearly six hours of double-timing through the forest and marshland, Sisko caught the chief's eye and flicked his gaze rearward . . . the signal O'Brien had waited for. Nodding, the chief began to drift to the rear. He drifted farther and farther back along the column until he found himself walking rear-guard next to Quark. After another half hour, long enough not to arouse suspicion, Captain Sisko joined him, followed fifteen minutes later by Worf.

"I instructed the colonel-mayor to continue following the riverbed," announced the war-worthy Klingon. "But perhaps I should remain at point and at least get them started correctly in battle."

Sisko sadly shook his head. "You have your orders, Worf. Win or lose, the Natives *must* experience what real battle tastes like. They must hate and fear it, even as they accept its terrible necessity."

Worf muttered something dark in Klingon, but O'Brien didn't catch it—and if the captain did, he ignored it.

The chief remained close enough not to lose contact with the entire column of two hundred heavily armed Natives, each man and woman carrying a weapon designed and built entirely by Native ingenuity, technology, and sweat. The column stopped so abruptly that O'Brien, straining his eyes left and right for an ambush, ploughed into the back of a woman whose name he didn't even know. Minutes later, Tivva-ma, daughter of the colonel-mayor, skipped gaily back to explain what was happening.

"Mom thinks—I mean, Colonel-Mayor Asta-ha says this is the bestest place to put in some of the pratfalls Owena-da designed."

"Pitfalls," corrected O'Brien absently, though he regretted it an instant later: kids said the cutest things, and there was plenty of time later for corrections.

Tivva-ma nodded soberly. "She wants to know if Colonel-Captain Sisko and Colonel-Commander Worf think that's all right. Izzit?"

The captain's mouth twitched, but he suppressed the smile that O'Brien could not. "The colonel-mayor has command. There is no need to ask permission . . . we are along as observers only."

Tivva-ma disappeared without another word, racing back up the column to pass along the approval (or lack of disapproval). A quarter of the Natives ghosted into the woods, whence the chief heard sawing and banging and bizarre grinding noises. The rest of the column resumed its march, leaving the engineer-sappers behind as reserves. *Clever,* thought O'Brien. *They've only read but one work on military tactics, something Worf was studying.*

As they approached the fine edge of the blue trees that marked the boundary between the forest and the wide pastureland surrounding three rivers, Odo came flapping back. The bird was ignored as he stepped behind a large bush. When the constable emerged, however, the Natives crowded around, wondering at the "new tech" that had brought him so far in the wink of an eye.

Odo hurried to Captain Sisko and conferred. Then the captain called a general meeting. "Gentlemen," he said, "we are about to make contact with the enemy. The Cardassians appear to have scanned the approaching Natives, and they're mobilizing for an assault."

"Sir," said the chief, "are they sending anyone toward the nearest power relay station?" The chief was asking, in a roundabout way, whether the Cardassians had yet figured out that the power was already out.

Sisko shook his head. "No, Chief, they're not; I believe we all understand the significance of that point."

Worf nodded. "There will be no surprise among the enemy. They already know they will encounter a different breed of Native. But perhaps they do not know how different."

"Let us hope," said the captain quietly. *Let us pray,* added O'Brien to himself.

Asta-ha did not have a tricorder, of course. But she sent a pair of the Vipers of Vanimastavvi—the new name for the commando brigade, replacing the Terrors of Tiffnaki—up tall trees, where they watched for the enemy approach. O'Brien had nothing to do but sit and wait, his least favorite activity.

Sitting, thinking, fretting, his *sang-froid* melted like frost in the morning sun. Soon he was trembling, but whether with excitement or fear he couldn't tell. The Natives seemed unaffected by the long wait.

Bastards probably don't even know enough to be scared, thought the chief ungenerously. *God, but I wish I were back with Keiko and Molly. I wonder whether these damned latinum-laced tree trunks will stop a Cardassian disruptor?*

He was about to find out, for at the very moment he was wondering about trees and distruptors, the lookouts whistled a warning—and the rest of the brigade promptly began the bizarre chorus of slithering whistles they used in place of applause. "Quiet! Quiet, damn you! This is an ambush, not a circus act!"

Eventually, they settled down, lying in wait as they had along the road during the training exercise, as the Cardassians approached slowly. *The trees will give partial cover for the numbers,* calculated the chief, *but the Cardies will definitely know something's up . . . especially since they have a Founder leading them.* Unbeknownst to them, or so Odo had reported—and O'Brien had no reason to disbelieve.

The Cardassians paused on the blue grass a hundred meters from the ambush to confer. From the disdainful looks they gave the forest every now and again, the chief decided they weren't too worried about the Native "wildlife" running berserk and attacking them. Then they formed a Cardassian Square: the front ranks dropped to their knees and aimed their disruptors, while the rear row aimed over their heads.

"Fire!" shouted the obviously "Cardassian" leader, who doubtless was the changeling. And fire they did. Sixty Cardassian energy weapons leaped the intervening distance like a spark jumping a gap, igniting explosions of splintered wood and sending flaming trees collapsing across the anticipated ambush, spraying dirt into Native faces—and directly killing nearly a dozen commandos whose cover was insufficient to protect them.

When the barrage ceased, the Cardassians stood and smugly returned their disruptor rifles to portarms to inspect the damage.

"Shoot back!" shouted Asta-ha . . . and the Natives remaining alive obeyed without hesitation. A dozen angry gasoline explosions assaulted O'Brien's eardrums from every direction. He squeezed as flat as he could, wrapping his hands across his head in a futile effort to protect himself from errant gas musketballs. The muskets used compressed gasoline vapor—a slight modification of the compressed-air blowgun of three days and several centuries ago—to fling round metal balls across a hundred meters with deadly accuracy and bone-shattering kinetic energy.

Simultaneously, a pair of flanks that had crept forward, forming a horseshoe-shaped line surrounding the Cardassians on three sides, opened fire with their own weapons. Tubes belched jellied gasoline, what used to be called *napalm*, at the uncomprehending Cardassians. Before the enemy could think of taking cover themselves, twenty had been slain, either cut in half by the twenty-five-milimeter musket balls or, even more hideously, burned to death by "Greek fire," as Sisko called it, that could neither be extinguished nor even scraped off the flesh.

The Cardassians screamed with rage and anguish and started to panic. But the leader—in the shape of a Cardassian colonel—shoved them forward instead of backward with a flurry of punches and well-aimed kicks. "Charge! Charge, you bloody fools, if you value your miserable lives!"

Cardassian training reasserted itself, and the troops rallied and ran forward, firing their disruptors in wide, sweeping arcs as they came. O'Brien swore lustily as one of the beams sliced through the top of a rock behind which he was crouching.

Now it was the Natives' turn to panic. They jumped up and bolted pell-mell—and the Cardassians cut down forty or fifty from behind, literally slicing them in half with full-power beams.

With a last glance back over his shoulder, O'Brien leaped to his feet, yanked Quark by the elbow, and ran back the way they had come.

But now a few of the Natives, probably the flankers, had turned and shot another volley at the charging Cardassians, mowing down another five to ten of them with the muskets . . . which were now empty, since they carried only two shots: the Natives had not invented autofeeding magazines quite yet. The troops around O'Brien flung their now useless muskets aside in order to run faster. Which they proceeded to do, passing the chief and Quark on both sides.

"Pump those legs, Quark, unless you want us to be in the very rear of a rearward advance!" The Ferengi didn't need to be told twice. O'Brien began to puff and wheeze, wishing he had spent more time in the gym and less time playing darts and fighting holo-suite battles with Julian Bashir.

My God, he thought, *Tivva-ma!* O'Brien pulled up, letting Quark run on ahead, and frantically searched for the little girl. Had she even survived? He felt such a physical blow in his stomach that he almost thought he might have been hit by some shrapnal. But then Owena-da dashed past, with Tivva-ma clinging to his back like a baby chimpanzee. Relieved, the chief resumed his tactical rearward advance, though now he was separated from everyone he knew. Quark had vanished into the forest as only a frightened Ferengi could.

They pushed deeper into the forest, and the Cardassians began to have problems: they were heavy shock troops, built not for speed but first impact. They stumbled over obstacles, both natural ones and those thrown down by fleeing Natives to slow the Cardassians' progress. The heavy battle armor the enemy wore worked to his disadvantage now, dragging him down in the swampy marshes and exhausting him in the pursuit.

O'Brien began to recognize a few landmarks. Suddenly remembering what the reserves had been doing, setting up deadly "pratfalls," he slowed to a walk, gasping for air and trying to spot anything that might be a trap. He was grabbed by one arm, and almost lashed out at his attacker, but then recognized her as Colonel-Mayor Asta-ha, Tivva-ma's mother and leader of the Vipers. "Come this way if you don't want to die," she said, matter-of-factly. Then she dragged him along an invisible ant-trail that she had no trouble following.

"Wait here. Let's see what new tech the girls and boys came up with, yes?" The middle-aged woman winked and loudly clicked her tongue, human-like gestures performed without the context of human subtlety, so that they looked stagey and out of place.

Grateful, O'Brien collapsed to his hands and knees, easily able to follow the Cardassians' progress by the bear-like thrashing through underbrush and low-hanging branches. Closer and closer they approached, to somebody's certain death . . . their own, or perhaps that of the Vipers of Vanimastavvi, or of five trivial Federation observers who very much hoped to live to observe another day.

CHAPTER 8

AS THE CARDASSIANS CHARGED, they began to disappear, one by one, like doves at a human magic show. Quark watched dumbfounded for several seconds, before he caught sight of a Cardassian soldier falling into a hole, squawking and flapping in indignation. Indignation that soon turned to shock and terror: the ground erupted with Natives on all sides, popping up from covered trenches and opening fire with their *firearms* at point-blank range.

Quark gagged and ducked, not wanting to see the results of a chemically propelled projectile striking a living (for the moment) body. "Rule of Acquisition Thirty-Five," he said to himself, "War is good for business." It didn't help; he was still terrified.

But a very un-Ferengi-like curiosity got the better of his sense of profit. *I've lived among the hu-mans too long,* lamented Quark. He couldn't help peeking over the edge of the chopped-down log behind which he cowered.

A huge tree-trunk swooped down from nowhere, dangling from a pair of cables. It swooshed over Quark's head—far over, but he ducked anyway—and smashed through the ranks of Cardassians, hurling dead and dying bodies fifteen meters through the air. There was a moment's awed silence; then the war resumed, and disruptor fire tore through a few defenders who had stopped to gawk at the carnage caused by one of their traps.

With a howl of outrage, a passel of Cardassians broke through the knots of Native fighters and charged directly toward Quark's position. The Ferengi curled up into the tightest cringe he could manage, desperately hoping they would recognize his surrender before killing him.

The scream of a blood-maddened Cardassian was enough to kick Quark into a hurried prayer to the Final Accountant . . . then the lead Cardassian broke through the brush and leapt over Quark's log—and directly over the small form huddled beneath it.

One after another, five soldiers dove across the log, not even one of them noticed the Ferengi. Astonished, Quark turned to watch them recede. They broke free and fled. They had no intention of renewing the fight, not this day!

Back in the fray, a series of horrible shrieks riveted Quark's attention. It sounded like a demon or monster of some new variety, and indeed *thak*-like shapes flashed through the gloom of the forest, about waist high to a Cardassian. Whatever the foul monsters were, they cut through the troops like twisty, crackly lightning bolts. It was several seconds before the Ferengi caught on that they were nothing but metal cables that had been attached to trees, and the trees bent double, so when released, they'd snap the cables like whips through the ranks.

Quark wrapped his arms over his lobes, desperately trying to shut out the ghastly sound of a hundred dead and dying. *This isn't what I signed up for! All I wanted was a little latinum, just a stake, a few hundred—I mean, a few thousand bars, just enough to show that bastard Brunt of the FCC that I'm a real Ferengi after all. . . .*

Just make it stop! Make it stop!

Quark slowly opened his eyes, unwrapping his arms. Profound silence filled the glade. Even the metallic croaking of the Sierra-Bravo birds had ceased. Late sunlight sliced through the torn overhead foliage, spotting the field of corpses with gold and blood-crimson, but nobody in all the clearing moved.

Quark rose shaking to his feet. He was terrified at the thought of being all alone among so many who had tallied their accounts and balanced their books, maybe even more than he had been at the tumult of battle. But it was over . . . wherever enemy attackers and Native defenders had taken their grudges, it was out of Quark's hearing.

"Did I pass out?" he asked aloud. It didn't seem to him that enough time had passed for them all to be so far. "Where is everyone?"

"Well, I, for one, am right behind you," said a too

familiar voice. Quark whirled to find himself confronted by an unruffled Constable Odo. "And no," said Odo, "you didn't pass out. You continued begging for mercy and cowering in true Ferengi fashion. The Grand Nagus would have been proud."

Quark wasn't sure what to make of the constable's response. His words were paying Quark a compliment, but the voice held an edge of sarcasm. "Uh, thanks, Odo," said the Ferengi, uncertainly.

"Quark," said Captain Sisko, pushing silently through the ferns and branches, "you did just fine. I certainly hope none of the away team actually participated in the battle. Did you?"

From nowhere, Worf and O'Brien materialized, each denying that he had done anything but hide and observe. Catching the flow at once, Quark smoothed his vest and jacket and agreed. "Of course, Captain. I carefully refrained from any fighting. The Cardassians will report seeing only Natives . . . ah, assuming any are still alive to report anything." But his voice still hid an unacceptable tremor.

As the away team moved around the glade, taking stock of the Native casualties, they slipped into and out of shadow, sometimes in direct sunlight, otherwise in blackness more complete because of the contrast. There were no Cardassian wounded or dead; they had taken all casualties with them when they retreated.

Sisko frowned, shaking his head. "There is ample credit for us all. And enough blame to put us on a prison colony for life. No, no," said the captain, waving his hands, "I am the only one at risk. None of you had a choice but to follow orders in time of war."

"Captain," said Worf, snuffing the ground like an animal, "the Cardassians left a trail a blind man could follow, and the—the Vipers are in pursuit. Shall we follow?"

Sisko was silent. Quark was surprised to see the imperturbable, immutable captain massaging his temples, wincing with pain. "No. Let them learn." Sisko looked up, staring along the trail. "We must leave soon—if the *Defiant* ever returns to orbit— and the Natives must look to their own defenses.

"The plan worked. There are at least thirty fallen comrades here, and another ten or fifteen back on the plains. We have taken some twenty percent casualties, not counting the walking wounded." The intensity of Sisko's glare made Quark turn his head and shuffle his feet.

"Then we have been successful," said Worf, nodding in satisfaction. He didn't appear to notice Captain Sisko's bitterness.

"My God," said Chief O'Brien, staring at each tall, lean, twisted corpse. "My God, doesn't it ever end? How many damned wars do I have to fight?" He sat down on a severed tree stump.

"Gentlemen," said the captain, gesturing them close. "Let us follow at a distance. When the Cardassians turn at bay and drive the Natives back, the survivors will flee into our arms, and we can doctor them as best we're able."

"And debrief them," said Worf with a peculiar pride. "And help them understand that they have become true blooded warriors at last." He grinned, and Quark suffered the hallucination that the Klingon's teeth were all filed to points, not beetle-biters like a Ferengi's, but huge and savage, like a human cannibal's.

The team pushed forward along the stomped and trampled underbrush and muddy swaths thick with bootprints. As Worf had said, even a Ferengi bartender could follow the path of pursuers and pursued—who would soon enough switch places yet again.

Quark dropped back even with O'Brien. "You know, Chief, you have a point." O'Brien said nothing. "It never does seem to end," said Quark, sighing.

They pushed on through dark mud, ducking from bright to dark. Somewhere at the back of the Ferengi's mind, he was vaguely aware that the very soil was thickly sprinkled with latinum. But—frighteningly—he no longer cared.

The dean erupted from the parabola and stalked forward, catching Kira by her biceps and propelling her to the turbolift shaft. They waited in silence until the turbolift returned, having disgorged its quasi-police passengers onto the Promenade. The dean and Kira entered, and without any words spoken, the turbolift dropped, then surged forward along one of the connecting tunnels from the core to one of the large transporter rooms. They rode in silence until the dean suddenly said, out of the blue, "No, do not take the ungrown prisoner. It may have been born in prison and never convicted."

Kira gasped, realizing that the dean must have been responding to a private communication—and she just happened to be standing close enough that her universal translator implant picked up the quiet response. He had just given Molly, at least, a reprieve; but what of Keiko?

"Dean," said Kira quickly, "if you will save the ungrown one, you must also save the female she clings to. She's the child's mother."

The dean turned his faceless head toward Kira, and the major felt a shudder that began in her bowels and finished in her heart. Then she heard a faint clicking, too soft for the universal translator to pick it up. *Prophets, please don't let him choose her,* Kira thought . . . then flushed with guilt, realizing that she had just inadvertently prayed for the deaths of two other Bajoran civilians.

As the turbolift whispered to a halt, and they stepped through the sliding doors of a circular corridor across the way from the transporter room, the final puzzle piece fell into place. *Convicted . . . he said Molly may never have been convicted!* With a flash of inspiration, every bizarre aspect of behavior of the "Liberated," every obscure reference, every incomprehensible misunderstanding became clear as cut dilithium.

The Liberated were former Dominion prison guards.

No wonder they fled, she thought, her mind racing. Knowing the Dominion's love of using certain races for specific tasks, they probably spent their entire lives in prison—though they'd never been convicted or sentenced—guarding those who had.

Everything fit: Prison guards were very much quasi-cops, as Garak had put it. And the misunderstanding about the "prisoners" in the bombardment shelters—*they must have thought they were in punishment cells. No wonder they put them back when they "escaped"!*

And these ex-prison guards were holding the entire station hostage . . . aliens who had lived their entire lives behind bars with only murderers and other felons for company. The thought chilled Kira's skin and made her scalp crawl. She said nothing, only following the dean, her knees feeling weak, and dreading what horrors she would see in the transporter room.

When they entered, two women that Kira recognized from the "jailbreak" stood on the transporter platforms. One demanded what was going to happen to her. The other, more realistically, was sobbing uncontrollably, on her knees begging for mercy. Kira remembered one of the girls, both younger than she, as one of Quark's Dabo dealers, Dalba Sin; she was the one on her knees. The other wore the uniform of the hydroponics division that Kai Winn had set up to replace the replicators, deemed too decadent for proper Bajorans. But Kira didn't know the young lady's name.

The executions occurred so fast Kira almost missed them. One of the prison guards reached down to the sobbing Dalba Sin as if picking her up. His hand briefly touched the back of the girl's head, and she pitched forward and lay unmoving. At the same time, another guard spun the demanding farmer around back to front, touched her cranium with a small, black-metal marble in his hand, and she, too, collapsed.

It was that swift. Kira didn't even have time to draw breath before both girls were being laid onto the platform, their arms crossed behind their backs. No torture, no joy on the part of the Liberated—unless it was the joy of remorseless efficiency. In the wink of an eye, two young girls had been murdered almost at Kira's feet . . . and there was nothing the major could do—or could have done—about it. "But—but you . . ." Kira fell silent; nobody was listening anyway.

A tide of hate such as she hadn't felt since the days of the Occupation seized her midbrain. She took a quick step toward the dean. "You son of—" It was as far as she got before the torc choked off her rage so strongly, she was certain her head was going to be sundered from her body.

Just before losing consciousness, Major Kira saw the dead bodies dematerialize from the transporter platform. *Now you know,* she thought, not sure to whom.

It took all of Kai Winn's self control not to shake, or cry, or pick up a knife and attack the nearest Faceless One, à la her young protege Kira Nerys. *Control the mind,* she remembered, *and the heart will follow.* Where had she heard that?

> *Control the breath, and the mind will follow*
> *Control the mind, and the heart will follow*
> *Control the heart, and peace will come upon you.*
> *Come, breath. Come, peace.*

Something something beats in tandem, puffing across the face of Bajor. A song, a poem, she had once . . .

Winn forced open her own eyes, willing herself to witness the deaths in the transporter room: she owed at least that to her flock. She didn't know the two young women by sight—there were so many—but she owed them at least a witnessing.

Then the bodies vanished, in that disconcerting way that Kai Winn still detested, though she had found occasion to violate the long-ago oath she'd sworn never to allow herself to be *transported* for fear she would leave her soul behind. The split-screen viewer still showed the *Harriman* on the right and the transporter room on the left, though the ship had not moved in several minutes and there was no more activity on the pad . . . only another Faceless One picking up Kira's limp body and removing it from the video frame.

Winn was certain her protégé was still alive. Nevertheless, the Kai prayed to the Prophets to shield young Nerys from harm.

Winn looked at the immobile Federation starship. *Now you know,* she thought without satisfaction. Well, perhaps a little. She watched the *Harriman* steadily, blinking so rarely that her eyes dried out and ached, then blurred, so she had to close them and wait for tears to moisten her vision back to clarity. She did not look round even when the dean returned to Ops to await response from Captain Taggart.

The Kai had patience. Besides, she was quite certain she knew what the response would be. The man was, after all, not a Bajoran. He simply was unprepared to deal with the "facts on the table," as the unbeliever Shakaar so bluntly put it after the Occupation.

The captain's face appeared so abruptly on the screen, so fast upon the heels of Kai Winn's own thoughts, that she inhaled sharply and took a step back. "This—this is an act of—of barbarous savagery," said the shaken captain. His face was distinctly pale, and sweat beaded his upper lip. Winn, like all grand negotiators and politicians, was an astute student of psychology; she would have counseled Captain Taggart to wait a few more minutes, mastering himself, before making his communication.

Taggart paused, but there was no response by the dean or any of the Liberated. The captain continued. "This is *not* over . . . not by a long shot. I protest in the strongest possible terms! This is unheard of, unconscionable. Have you, at last, no decency left? No regard for intelligent life? You call yourselves the Liberated, but you have no respect for anyone else's liberty. The entire quadrant is watching, and they will know you for beasts if you continue this—this *murder.* I demand an immediate end to these executions . . . don't you understand the first rules of negotiation?"

"Your time has expired," said the dean of the dead at last. "We shall now execute another pair of prisoners."

Captain Taggart's transmission ended before the man could be seen reacting to the threat. Winn was not in the least surprised to see, a few instants later, the *U.S.S. Harriman* back hurridly away from the station. The ship dwindled until it was a gray dot, then a black point, then gone altogether, its gigantic hull too far away to be discerned by the viewer on normal magnification.

Not in the least surprised, but angry: angry at a tenuous, vague, ambiguous Federation that spent more time dithering and wringing its hands than it spent pursuing comprehensible policy objectives. Angry at this arrogant man who had inserted himself into a delicate situation, grabbing hold of a fragile flower hard enough to crush it and then simply dropping it to the ground like a guilty child. Bitter at a duplicitous, quadrant-wide authority with no real hegemony, an authority that turned its back on its *own agreements* whenever they became inconvenient. Despairing of another year of peace for Bajor, and fearful that the Prophets were angered by all the secular wrangling of Shakar and his ill-mannered revolutionaries and by the diminished faith of the modern Bajoran.

"The starship has departed," said the dean.

With a wrench, Kai Winn realized he was talking to her. "Yes, m'lord. They have left."

"We require only the portable, far-seeing anomaly. We have no desire to execute more prisoners."

"Yes, m'lord. Your restraint buoys our spirits."

"We have searched for the anomaly, what you call the Orb. We know it is on this station. Bring us the Orb, and we shall depart, and you shall once more enjoy liberty, as we do."

"I have located it, m'lord. There are certain . . . political difficulties. But I . . ." Winn paused. *Oh Beloved Prophets—dare I go through with it?* She

113

swallowed hard. "My lord, I would do anything to save my people, my flock. *Anything.* I will—" she forced the words through her throat—"I will bring you the portable, far-seeing anomaly, the Orb, within the day." *May the Prophets forgive my lie. But what else can I say?*

She turned a furious visage to the dean. "Then you will leave. You will leave us alive and in peace. You will never return." Winn betrayed no particle of duplicity; but the dean would never, she vowed, get within touching distance of an Orb.

The dean rotated his head in a circle. "We accept your terms. Bring us the anomaly, and we shall leave immediately."

Feeling a wave of nausea—*stress,* she decided—Kai Winn left Ops for the turbolift. She had a desperate need to return to her stateroom . . . and her dark and desperate dreams: for the Prophets had a story for Winn to hear, and she must not disappoint.

CHAPTER
9

THIRTY YEARS AGO

BEING STRIP-SEARCHED was not high on Sister Winn's list of fun things to do of an evening. On the contrary—it was the most bitterly humiliating thing that had ever happened to her. The only thing that made it bearable was the sly knowledge that the Prophets had whispered prophecy in her ear, and she had already dumped the holocamera—into Gul Ragat's own backpack. As the Cardassian carried the pack (or had a noncommissioned officer carry it for him) merely for show, and never actually dug into it for anything, Winn was reasonably confident the camera would not be found. But if it were, it would mean her swift but painful death—or else transportation up to the new orbital torture chamber, *Terok Nor.*

She turned her gaze within, upon her own soul and her omnipresent Guides and Avatars, the

Prophets; she was not even in attendance upon her naked and humiliated body. Two corporals of the guard and one private soldier, none of whom she knew, led the search, and of course they found the trick bootheel and the money she had stashed there. They made no comment, merely dropping the Bajoran bills into a plastic, self-sealing, evidence bag for subsequent interrogation. The rest of her clothing was free of any incriminating evidence. They returned her priestly robe, torn and stretched, and handed her back the jacket she wore, inside-out. They did not return her shoes.

Without a word, she reassembled her garments and sat barefoot on the hard ground of the tent floor, trying to look miserable, waiting for "her Gul" to return and decide what to do. Looking wretched was not difficult in her present circumstance. But she held tight to the lifeline of memory: *the holocam is safe, the pictures of the control room and military codes are well hidden.*

Exhaustion overwhelmed Sister Winn. She let her head fall upon her folded arms and dozed fitfully. Dreadful nightmares befouled her rest: she was a hunted hare, driven to the ends of the earth by long-fanged hounds with gigantic trapezius muscles.

She awoke hours later to find herself lying on her side, curled into a foetal position, shivering with the cold. She had no blanket. The Cardassians had left the priestess unbound, but a guard stood outside the tent flap, and the material of the tent itself was some artificial fabric that was breathable but uncuttable— even if she'd had a knife.

Winn was puzzled for a moment. *What awakened*

me? Then she heard the voice she most dreaded at that moment, speaking in Cardassian.

"Wise if you'd just leave off and take another watch, Mata."

"If I leave my post . . ."

"I will take full responsibility. You're in my chain of command, so you have no choice"

Winn sat up slowly, so as not to set her head spinning. She recognized the voice of the bully-guard, the corporal who had been humiliated by the sergeant—and one of the guards who had stripped her.

Winn stood, dreading the worst. The tent flap opened, and a grinning goblin entered.

The corporal was tall for a Cardassian; he had to hunch over to duck his head under the tent flap. His eyes were unintelligent, sadistic marbles of black. Winn could not even see the white around the pupils; they were solid, like a reptile's. He kept his hands low as he crouched, and his finger-ends dragged along the ground for a moment, leaving tracks.

Winn backed away from the apparition, but her shoulders swiftly brushed against the tent wall. There was nowhere to go, no way out but through the ghostly guard.

"I believe you know what happens next," he said, a peculiar grin on his lips that at first Winn didn't recognize. Then she realized that it was the same look a man gives a loose woman he's about to debauch. He ran a swollen, pink tongue across his lips, moistening them.

Winn said nothing. Her mind was blank. A fist of

fear squeezed her heart until her whole chest ached. Her own lips were dry as old bone.

"If you scream or yell," added the corporal unnecessarily, "you will not enjoy the consequences."

He clenched his fist so hard, the knuckles cracked. Winn tried to swallow, but she had no saliva. She noticed he had a knife, a ceremonial Dagger of Maqatat. He could not have earned it himself, not being a gentleman nor even a commissioned officer. *It must be his father's or grandfather's,* she thought, wondering why the thought should be important when she was about to be beaten, violated, or worse.

"The Gul won't like it if you damage me," she said. It sounded unconvincing even to her ears, but she persevered. "He's furious at me now. Thinks I betrayed him, but I didn't! When he comes to himself, I'll be his favorite again, and he won't like it that you, you, you hurt me, especially if you leave me dead!"

The corporal laughed like brass knuckles against a mouth full of Bajoran teeth. "Dead? I would never slay such a beauty as yourself."

The corporal took two swift strides and caught Winn by the sleeve of her habit. He had a scar across his forehead, bisecting the spoon-shaped bone ridge that gave Cardassians their Bajoran epithet. Winn exerted all her will power not to flick her eyes downward at the Dagger of Maqatat; she knew where it was without looking.

The Prophets guided Winn's hand. Feeling Their hands on hers, she deftly plucked the dagger from his belt-sheath, even more spritely than she had slicked Neemak Counselor's pocket. The corporal realized in a flash what she had done, and he leapt back almost too quickly for her to follow. Rapist he may have been, but he was a soldier first.

"Well, I see you have a bite! But truly, what can you do with one little knife?"

Winn's mind raced faster than ever it had before. She knew she could not possibly hope to best this brute in single combat. His bare knuckles and feet would disarm her in the moment she attacked, and he would truly hurt her then. So what was she to do? What was Their plan for her?

The corporal edged forward, extending his left hand while keeping his right in reserve. He was reaching slowly, inexorably for the dagger. The priestess had but one moment to act, else she would be disarmed and at the mercy of a merciless, enraged pain machine.

Then the rest of the plan popped into her head, fully formed, like Benetheas springing from the belly of her father, M'theo Niisil. Sister Winn stepped away from the monster and pressed the blade sharp-end first at her own breast, directly above her heart. "No, my lord," she answered, voice barely audible past the fear. "My plan is much darker. If you take one more step, if you don't leave this tent immediately, I'll *kill myself.*"

"What? What the—"

"I'll plunge this dagger into my heart. Everyone will recognize the Dagger of Maqatat. The private knows you were here. He'll tell Gul Ragat. The sergeant will remember what you said. No one will believe that you didn't do it."

His mouth worked, but no words came out. He

stared, dumbfounded, struggling to comprehend this damned peculiar turn of events.

"You think you can simply pluck the dagger back and run from here. But they know you were here. They'll perform microscopic analysis on the wound and find traces of metal; the metal will perfectly match your dagger. You won't be able to escape, Corporal."

"You—you—!"

"Nothing to say? Then I'll say it for you. They'll say you murdered me, and the Gul will blame you for everything. He'll say your mindless homicide prevented him from questioning me himself."

Winn had regained control of her voice, but she lowered it nearly to a whisper, grabbing the corporal's attention as a shout would have lost it. She kept her eyes on her enemy, but his own gaze flickered uncontrolled from Winn to the tent flap and back to the dagger. "You know what they can do," she continued, smiling. "You've been to *Terok Nor*. You'll get to go back . . . but as one of *us* this time. Now get out of here."

The corporal stared, doing nothing. He was frozen between consternation and fear for his own career, even his life. He *had* been up; he did know what "they" could do.

Winn clenched her teeth and shoved the dagger into her own chest, just a touch, a mere finger's width. She gasped at a pain more savage than anything she had ever felt before. The agony should have stopped her, but the Prophets had seized control of her mind and hand. She was resolved. "I am not bluffing," she said, choking. "If you don't get out this instant, in the next, I shall be dead with your bloody dagger in my breast."

He started to back away toward the tent flap, but not fast enough to suit the priestess. *"Go!"* she screamed, startling him out of his torpor.

With an unintelligible stammer, he turned and fled.

He was gone, and Sister Winn could collapse to the floor, pressing her hand over her bloody, bleeding chest. She held onto the dagger, but the corporal never returned.

Jadzia Dax tried bitterly hard to keep a smile on her lips; behind it, her teeth were clenched so hard her jaw began to ache. She tried not to grip the sides of her seat too obviously. Surely, Bashir knew his own piloting abilities, but she marveled at the speed and dexterity he showed. I wonder what they're teaching in medical schools nowadays, she thought, as the doctor continued his ambitious maneuvers with the Native skimmer.

Bashir seemed to relish putting the car onto the deck, foot-dragging distance off the dirt, and whipping right through shallow, winding canyons, leaving rooster-tails on the small rivers that carved them, and then, without slacking speed, sailing directly into sparse, gray-blue forests, sometimes even right *under* large tree branches . . . all at speeds that Dax insisted on imagining as half-impulse or even warp one, though they probably were no more than fifty or sixty meters per second. Fast enough! She thought twice that her heart was going to stop, if it ever dropped back down out of her throat.

"Nice—nice—nice day for a leisurely stroll—eh, Julian?" she said.

"Don't distract the pilot when he's driving. I'm sorry, what did you say?" Bashir turned his head to look fully at Dax.

"The tree! Julian, *look out!*" But Bashir swerved expertly around the tree, having already mapped it in his mind before pulling his little prank on her. Dax sighed deeply, resigning herself to being splattered to assuage the doctor's ego. "All right, Julian, I apologize for the A, B, D thing. It's just that I know Ben better than any of you, and as Curzon, I fought with my Klingon swordmates against the Cardassians more times than I can count, and I just *know* how they'll line up—I can't explain it any better than that!"

"Oh, I know," said Bashir, again watching where he was going. "I'm not angry, Jadzia. I'm just nervous about the captain and the rest of the team." Bashir frowned, and for a moment Dax forgot to be frightened; something was truly worrying him.

"I'm sure they can synthesize something or other to help against the cyanogens in the air," she said. "And they're not stupid enough to drink the local water or eat the food. They'll do the same thing we're doing, steal from the Cardassians."

Bashir pressed his lips tightly together. An internal battle raged, and Dax had no idea what was going on behind those dark eyes. After a protracted period of silence, he spoke. "I never expected us to stay this long in the atmosphere of Sierra-Bravo, Jadzia. The—my compound—Dax, *nothing* the captain could whip up can fully protect from the cyano-mutagenic damage for very long. Nothing I could manufacture would do it, not without a full medical lab and a few years more research."

"What are you saying? What's your diagnosis, Doctor?"

"For us humans, Trill, and Klingons, there is a limit to the time we can spend on this planet—I'm sure Odo will be fine, and I don't know about Quark. After that limit is reached, irreversible pulmonary-tissue damage begins. The lungs can be replaced . . . but within a short period, just a few hours, after the lungs start bleeding—allowing unmediated cyanogens into the bloodstream—cardiac and neural damage will occur."

"You're saying we could be—brain-damaged?"

"Loss of motor skills and nausea are the first symptoms. Eventually, vision becomes difficult, the patient sees flashes and auras. Cortical shutdown and memory loss, finally death . . . after a certain point, there is nothing modern medicine can do about it."

Dax inhaled sharply. She could not stop herself from performing a mental "level-three diagnostic" on her own cortical functions, imagining the worst. She held her hand out, looking for trembling, and felt a wash of panic when she saw that she was unable to hold it steady.

"Oh, don't be so melodramatic," said Bashir angrily. "Don't you think I'd know if you were suffering from the breakdown yet?"

She flushed guiltily. "Sorry, Julian. I can live with

a lung or heart replacement, natural or artificial. But when you start talking about neural damage, my you-know-what clenches."

Bashir took the skimmer up a little higher, risking detection by Cardassian scanner crews. "I'm sorry, Jadzia. This has been weighing on my mind for some days now. I'm. . . ." He looked at her again, but they were above the ground terrain, and Dax was more relaxed. "I'm not casting aspersions on the captain, but I don't think his jerry-rigged cyanogen-protecting compound is going to be as effective as mine. And that means the away team's time limit is closer than ours—they're farther along the destruction cycle, I just don't know how far."

"And what is this time limit you keep talking about? How long do we have, how long do they have?"

Bashir shook his head and turned back to his driving. He dropped back down, whipping into another snakey canyon, another gut-tightening series of twists and turns. *He doesn't have a clue,* Dax thought to herself; *and if Julian doesn't know, nobody knows.*

"This neural damage," she said after a few moments; "how much warning do you get?"

"If you spot the symptoms, a couple of days, maybe as many as four. But Captain Sisko doesn't even know what to look for."

Dax nodded silently, no longer grudging Bashir his not-so-excessive speed.

"Dax," he said, after his own long pause, "the other thing I wanted to mention was that—"

The Native skimmer abruptly dropped from the

sky. Dax screamed, while Bashir's face was frozen in shock at the sudden loss of power and imminent crash. The commander braced herself against the impact.

It made no difference. They were skimming through a gorge, twenty meters off the ground, and when the power cut off, the craft veered precipitously, following a ballistic path into the mud alongside the sluggish river. Dax was thrown clear instantly, yanked out of her seat as if by a giant's hand. She struck the mud heavily, sliding for such a long distance on her belly that she actually had time to think she might be able to regain control. At that moment, something caught her arm and set her rolling.

She lost count of how many complete revolutions her body made before finally sliding to a stop, feet first, against the wreckage of the Native skimmer. Bashir was still in his seat, pinned by the exercise-bar motion controller. Even from her prone position, lying on her back and looking up dazedly, she could tell that he had a fractured leg. A *compound* fracture, with a piece of white bone sticking right up through the flesh—through the cloth of his pseudo-native costume—and smirking wickedly at her.

Her head still spun, and only the fact that she was facing the sky told her which way was up. Dax tried closing her eyes, but that was worse: her head spun like a Dabo wheel, and she whimpered and opened her eyes again.

Several seconds passed before she could stand. All the while an urgent voice shrieked in her head to hurry, hurry, Julian was bleeding to death! But when she finally struggled to her feet to examine him, he wasn't bleeding all that badly. His breathing was raspy, but he was conscious and holding his hand over the wound, exerting pressure.

"Dax," he croaked; "Dax—are you—all right?"

"Julian, I'm fine, I think. Wait. . . ." She twisted her head left and right, up and down, in a circle; then she probed her belly and sides with a stiff finger, hunting for a sharp pain that might indicate internal injuries. The mud-sliding had saved her: she was clean, but filthy. *And filthy rich, if I never wash these clothes,* she thought dazedly, remembering the latinum content of the soil.

Gingerly, Dax took the doctor's hand away from the wound. It still didn't bleed heavily. The bone shard only stuck a centimeter and a half through the skin, and it looked relatively clean, no splinters. "Julian," she said, tiptoeing around the delicate subject, "I have to, ah, set this, don't I?"

Bashir winced in pain, unable to speak. He nodded raggedly.

"I hate to tell you this, Julian, but you're going to have to talk me through it. I've done some doctoring in my time, mostly Klingon blood brothers who got a little rambunctious after hours, but I've never dealt with a compound fracture of the—the tibia?"

"Femur," said the doctor through gritted teeth. "You have—to grab below—knee—pull. Hard. Really—really hard."

"Are you, um, going to pass out?"

"Prob—probably."

"Then what?"

"Makes it—easier. Keep pulling. Pull straight.

Keep pressure—keep pulling—pressure. Oh God."
Another spasm of pain tore across Bashir's face.

Act fast, said the voice in Dax's brain, *while he's already hurting. Let him go out fast!*

Moving quickly but precisely, she took hold of the doctor's leg and with a swift but smooth pull, tugged it outward. Julian Bashir moaned, and as advertised, passed out from the agony. Dax continued to tug, taking advantage of the respite. She pulled with her right, while the fingers of her left hand pulled the torn flesh and cloth aside and pushed the bone back through the wound.

Her stomach clenched at the sight. She had dressed many a *bat'telh* slice, none of which had affected her much. But the sight of white bone sticking up through raw, red meat nauseated her so much that when Dax finally felt the bone rotate back into place, she leaned away and lost the undigested remnants of her last meal. She was thankful she had eaten only a light breakfast.

After evacuating the contents of her stomach, Dax sat back and continued to pull on the leg, keeping the bone ends from grating against one another. The foul taste in her mouth nauseated her further, but she had nothing left to lose.

After five sweat-soaked, sour-tasting minutes, Bashir finally limped back to consciousness. He raised his head, trying to see his leg.

"It's still there," said Dax in a bitter humor; "I didn't have to amputate."

"My bag," said the doctor. "Orthopedal stimulator. Looks like—saltshaker—teal."

Dax scanned the ground with her eyes, finally

spotting the doctor's shoulder bag. Stretching out her left arm while still holding tight with the right, she retrieved the open bag. There were only two medical instruments left; one was a hypospray, and the other did not look like a teal saltshaker.

"Um, Julian, I think we're in trouble. Will this thing help?" She held up the unknown item, which was a dark-blue thimble.

Bashir squinted, then sighed, shaking his head.

"What's in the hypospray?" she asked, hopeful.

"Anti—viral, antibacterial—all purpose—antiseptic. Give one amp."

Catching her tongue between her teeth, Dax sprayed the antiseptic directly into Bashir's leg, just above the wound. "All right, you're not going to get gangrene. Now what?"

"Find the ortho—orthopedal stimulator."

"Julian, there's wreckage scattered across a square kilometer of canyon! There's no way I can find it in less than a full day, and you need help *right now*. Come on, kiddo; think back. How did the ancient doctors fix broken legs in the premedical age?"

Bashir said nothing for a solid minute, and Dax was afraid she'd lost him again. Then he grunted. "Splint," he said. "Get two sticks. Thick. Something to tie them with."

Finding sticks wasn't difficult. There was plenty of kindling scattered among the trees at the bottom of the gorge. Dax gently lay the doctor's leg down on the opposite seat of the skimmer, feeling a wash of guilt as Bashir hissed in pain. She scurried off, rustled up several likely candidates for the splint, and rushed back.

At Bashir's instruction, Dax carefully laid the sticks on either side of his broken leg, the bottom ends actually sticking down below his foot by six centimeters or so. Then she tied the splint tightly with cords pulled from her own Native-style cloak, one cord below the foot, the others at various places up the leg. By this time, Bashir was sitting up and helping, though it didn't take a Betazoid to feel the doctor's pain. Dax still winced every time she looked at the angry, red wound just above Bashir's knee.

"What happened to the power?" asked the doctor, startling Dax out of her nauseated reverie.

"Huh? Oh." Her tricorder had miraculously survived, probably because she had dissipated so much momentum by sliding along the slick mud. She set the pickups to detect power potential instead of actual power and scanned 360 degrees around.

"Nothing . . . and nothing. There's no power potentia anywhere." Dax was silent for a moment, remembering the last time she had observed such a phenomenon. "Julian," she said at last, "you know this is exactly the typical Cardassian attack: first they kill the local power, then they strike against the helpless, dumbfounded Natives who can't figure out why all their new tech has suddenly stopped working."

Bashir bit his lip, then mastered himself again. "Can you scan for Cardassians, Jadzia?"

"Already recalibrating, even as we speak." She repeated the slow scan all about the compass, not liking what she saw.

"Nothing. Nobody. Nowhere." She sat, thinking

about being stranded, starving to death, her bones someday being found leaning back against a rock, the leg-bones crossed nonchalantly. "Well, Julian, what now?"

"Find the—orthopedal stimulator."

"One ortho-stim, coming up."

But it didn't. Days passed, and Dax never did find the stimulator, or much of anything useful and undamaged except the Cardassian food and water still strapped to the remains of the passenger cage.

Dax tried to keep track of the time, but she grew confused, unable to remember whether she had scratched a mark on the rock each morning or not. *It's been at least ten days,* she remembered thinking one evening. When all there was to do was talk, one day or one night seemed much like another.

She wanted to move, to head toward Benjamin Sisko—or where she thought he might be—however many hundreds of kilometers that was. They had crashed in a direct line between the observed Cardassian spoor and where she extrapolated Sisko's position, so there was some hope that he might be coming closer to them, assuming the captain intended to take the battle to the enemy. She wanted to join up with Sisko before the battle, so they wouldn't be caught between hammer and anvil.

But Julian couldn't move, not yet. *A few more days,* she promised, keeping a nervous eye on the food, and especially the water. "Damn," she groused, "I wish I hadn't let you talk me into giving that bloody Gul four man-weeks of supplies."

"Well, who knew we were going to run out of gas?"

said the doctor. His spirits seemed up, and he was itching—literally—to try hobbling on a crutch.

Then, on a day she had seriously considered taking Julian for his first practice stroll—his raw-meat wound looked *much* better, definitely uninfected—she chanced to stand on a rock and make another slow, 360-degree scan.

"Whoops," she said, "company. Well, that was inevitable."

"The Cardassians?"

Dax nodded. "A couple of hundred or so. Thataway." She indicated by pointing. "And moving in our direction. Why now? Why not next week, when we wouldn't even be here?" Bashir rightly guessed it was a rhetorical question, and didn't answer.

She continued. "Oh, and while we're at it . . ." She recalibrated once again and scanned for human/Ferengi/Klingon DNA. "Yes, of course, that figures! Looks like we finally found the captain and the away team, and a whole mess of Natives, about nine kilometers yonder"—she pointed in the opposite direction—"and heading in fast."

Dax snapped off the tricorder and tucked it back in its padded case. "Good news, Julian: your leg is better. We were just going to leave, but instead we're about to be standing at ground zero of Armageddon between the forces of good and the forces of evil." She smiled brightly. "At least we're not going to be lonely." She sat heavily next to the doctor, chin in hands, wondering how she was going to manage this reunion without the pair of them becoming Cardassian trophies.

CHAPTER
10

A FURTIVE MEETING. Darkness in the corridor . . . Major Kira brushed past the station tailor without so much as a sideways glance. She felt nothing. *Should I have?* But Garak coughed delicately after they passed, and Kira hoped and prayed. Darkness again, and solitude. The moment passed—and hours would pass before Kira could return to her stateroom (her "cell," as the dean would have it) to rest—rest and feel gently in her pocket to find what she hoped was the offspring of that furtive meeting in the dark, lonely corridor.

Just a sliver, the merest speck of metal. But using a mirror, she fit it perfectly into the slight, hairline crack between the edges of the torc, the slave collar.

She thought to test it, but thought a second time. Alarms, perhaps. A diagnostic message broadcast to the Liberated, the prison guards who controlled

Emissary's Sanctuary, which Kira was already in her heart gloomily calling *Deep Space Nine* again.

The sliver would remain untested, nestled inside the collar, waiting for the ultimate test. *My life is in the hands of that bastard spoon-head spymaster,* she thought. *May the Prophets help us all!*

The summons bell chirped in Kira's cell, rescuing her from a sleep so deep, a dream so dire, that she could remember nothing, despite being interrupted in the middle . . . nothing but the horrific sense of billions of kilos of water pressing upon her from all sides, crushing her young body like a bug between two palms. She swam awake, leaping to her feet with such alacrity that she shamed herself. "Kira," she said, coughing up saliva that went down the wrong way.

"You will come to the central command center," said the dean without preamble. The transmission ceased. What explanations need be offered to a slave?

When Kira rode the turbolift into Ops, she was shocked to see Kai Winn standing at the monster's left hand. The woman looked old, head bowed, lips pressed together in tight surrender, the peaked mitre on her head drooping, as if even the cloth itself were tired of resisting. Winn stared at the deck, not even glancing up when Kira stomped from the turbolift. *She can't face me,* realized the major in wonder. *Oh Prophets, what have you done, my Kai?*

"The portable, far-seeing anomaly has been located," said the dean—this was more than was strictly necessary, but he had come to trust his slave.

His black, featureless face *looked* at Kira, and a shiver danced along her spine. "You will retrieve it. The chief of prisoners will tell you where."

Kira edged closer, stepping from the platform, passing Chief O'Brien's engineering well, coming to rest just by the science console, her fingers lightly touching the cool plastic. "Kai?" she asked, voice trembling, "is this true?"

"I have offered, my child. There are lives."

"It's an *Orb,*" said the major firmly, with finality.

"It's a hundred lives, child. More."

Bile exploded up Kira's throat. She swallowed, feeling herself so close to tears that she turned her own face away, lest they actually fall. Her mind refused to function. What was there to do? The offer had been made and accepted. If Kira didn't run fetch the Orb, another would . . . and to what avail?

"May the Prophets forgive us," said someone— was it Kai Winn or Kira herself? The major could not be sure.

"Child—"

"Where?"

"Child. . . ."

She wants to be forgiven, this Kai. Rot in hell before you gain sanction from me, traitor! "Where is it, Kai Winn?"

Winn stood silent a long moment. The dean displayed infinite patience, perhaps realizing the depth of emotion that tore the two women. "Down," said the old woman at last. "Down as far as you can go. Among the engines and reactors—I don't under-stand the machinery, and I don't remember exactly where I was told it was hidden. But you will find it, child. You've seen it many times."

"I have seen it in the *temple,* Kai." Kira stressed the word perhaps overmuch, but she meant it to burn.

"Please bring it to me here in Ops. I will give it with my own hands to the dean. The Liberated will leave, restoring the station to Bajor and leaving us in peace."

"You will leave now," commanded the dean.

Kira was about to comply when the rage, long suppressed by the collar and the self-censorship it enforced, burst through the stopcock in Kira's throat. "You will die now," she said, matter-of-factly and without audible emotion. She spoke with the certainty of a Prophet.

With no more ado, Major Kira reached across the science console to a ratageena mug that had lain unregarded since the occupation began. She took it by the handle; as yet no one—not the dean, the Kai, or any of the guards—had parsed Kira's last prophecy.

Kira held the cup firmly and punched it into the edge of the console. The breakproof plastic shattered nicely, leaving her holding a jagged shard attached to the handle. She stepped forward briskly, and at last the assembly began to react.

"Kira, child!" exclaimed Winn, stepping back in startled alarm. The guards lurched forward, caught off balance by the smoothness of the strike.

Even reaction time half that of a Bajoran's couldn't protect against a complete surprise attack.

DAFYDD AB HUGH

The dean himself stumbled backwards, bumping into the communications console and raising his hands in obvious consternation. *So they can be defeated,* she thought dully, *taken by surprise and scared.*

No one anticipated her attack. No one was close enough to respond on the fly. Before another breath could be drawn by any of the parties, Kira had pressed the sharp, jagged piece of plastic against the dean's throat, taking him by the breastplate to prevent escape. "You will die," she repeated, "if you touch this Orb. You will die if you do not release us. You will die if you do not get the *hell* off *my station,* this instant."

Kira's heart was pounding like a tiny *bickett* with fear and rage . . . but the collar, she realized, was inert; Garak had done his job well. She could not be stopped. The dean must only now be realizing he had lost all control.

If he was, he was also doing a good job of hiding that realization. The dean made no move, no attempt to wrestle the jerry-rigged knife from her grasp; nor did the two guards take more than a single step toward the pair before stopping, presumably at the dean's silent orders, and withdrawing to the periphery of Ops.

"I'm not bluffing," said Kira, staring into the inky blackness of the dean's alleged face. *Is it his face? Or is it a helmet after all?* It looked too glassy to be flesh.

"We anticipated this sign of independence and ingenuity," said the dean quietly, without emotion. "We have prepared escape insurance. Behold."

Some force of certain knowledge made Kira turn

136

her head, careful not to let the knife slip from its target. The turbolift had vanished. But a few tense moments later, it whispered back into Ops.

The lift held five passengers: one guard, Jake Sisko, and three Bajorans. All prisoners but the last wore terrified expressions and a large, red nodule taped to their throats. Jake stood behind them all.

"Please inform Major Kira what has been done," said the dean.

Keiko looked too horrified to make a sound. Jake swallowed hard and spoke, his voice sounding a lot calmer than he must have felt, from what Kira could see. "These—these things are explosives," he said. "That's what the guards said. They say they'll blow our heads off if you don't do whatever they tell you." The last words created such a look of disgust and self-loathing on Jake's face that Kira's heart broke. What could the poor boy—the young man—do? He was stymied.

"We shall execute the prisoners if you do not disarm yourself and retrieve the far-seeing anomaly."

Kira's hand began to shake, from inner tension and from the physical letdown. She had hungered for the final battle, only to have the chair yanked away when she sat at the victor's table. After a long, silent argument without words, Kira's arm fell limp. She dropped the makeshift knife to her side . . . then dropped it completely onto the floor. She did not let go of the dean's armor; indeed, she could not will her fingers to relax. But one of the guards strode forward and yanked her away.

"There must be punishment," said the dean, "or

other prisoners will riot." Then he stepped back, out of the way, while the two guards moved close to Kira.

She knew what was coming. Still, the first blow was a surprise, a short jab to her solar plexus. It punched the wind right out of her lungs, spasming her diaphragm so she could not even draw a breath. Then the real beating began.

Kira Nerys had been beaten before; nobody in the Occupation could have completely escaped physical torture at the hands of Gul Dukat and some (but not all) of the other Cardassians. But this brutal punishment was as professional as anything ever dished out by the Cardassian goons of *Terok Nor*.

Kira tried to tense her muscles and cover her head and chest as best she could, but the Liberated were experts at finding the weak point, the unguarded spot, and driving their shell-hard fists into the woman's flesh. They did not allow her to lose consciousness, never striking where she would be knocked out or killed. A stomp from an armored boot broke most of the bones in Kira's left hand. She lost a tooth to a particularly vicious finger-strike.

The pain was exquisite. Her eye was swollen shut, and she never did recover her breath. She resolved not to make a sound; but that pious hope was quickly dashed, and she heard herself whimpering like an animal, unable to stop the bleating: the alien prison guards knew exactly which buttons of humiliation to push to break her down farther than mere pain could have done.

They didn't ask her a single question; but after a

number of blows disoriented her, she started mumbling her name, rank, and province, alternately aware of where she was and believing herself to be back on Bajor during the Troubles. The Liberated paid her words no attention. They were interested not in information but in punishment.

But at last it was over. Broken and sobbing, nose running, it took Major Kira ten minutes at least to pick herself up again, first to knees, then to her feet. She looked first to the hostages: Jake's face was frozen in a mask of hatred so deep, he looked more like his father than did Sisko himself. Keiko's was turned away; she couldn't look. Molly had buried her face in her mother's side.

I survived. I will survive. I am survival. Without asking again, Kira stumbled up the platform to the turbolift. "Lefel—lefel thir'y-fife." The very bottom, where six reactors squatted, three of them currently live.

It was hard to talk around the missing tooth and the blood in her mouth. The turbolift dropped silently, uncaring, through the bowels of the station, heading for the three bound suns that ran *Deep Space Nine* and the heavily shielded room that contained them, where the bulkheads were so thick that even sensors could not penetrate to find the small box with a window to the Prophets.

Winn was right. It had been the perfect hiding place. *Too damn bad,* thought Kira, holding onto the railing to keep from falling to the floor.

Edging from the turbolift into the generator room, the throbbing from the hulking reactors shook Kira, an ogre grabbing a knee in each hand and yanking rhythmically twice a second. Her head pounded in unison, though the Liberated guards had mostly avoided it during their "extrajudicial punishment," striking her face only a few times, mostly by accident. Even her remaining teeth rattled with the *whump, whump* of the huge fusion generators.

Dropping slowly to knees and one hand was a relief, justified by the need to find the Orb. She crawled along the floor, hampered by her broken left hand, eyes still tearing in reaction to the brutality, lips swollen and split, oozing blood. At last—*too soon!*—she found the familiar box with the cabinet door. For several moments, lying on the floor and feeling the pulse of unimaginable power rock her and throw off the balance so fragilely regained, she contemplated the blessed Orb. She needed to rest; she needed time to think.

There was no way out, no loophole by which she could fail to retrieve the Orb and prevent anyone else from bringing it back, even Kai Winn herself. *I had my shot. I failed. Perhaps the Kai's way is best, after all.* At last, Kira reverently gathered up the box in a one-armed hug of unbearable tenderness, feeling the twice-each-second vibration as the pulse of the Prophets.

But as she rose, something tickled the back of her bruised brain, something not quite right. Something *felt* wrong. Even the box of Orb itself felt wrong; everything was wrong.

But Kira was just too sick and tired to fight, fret, or fume about certain negligible differences in the Orb she had loved before. Rising unsteadily, Kira stumbled back aboard the turbolift and headed back up to Ops, cursing as every passing level brought the holiest of holies closer to the hands of profane barbarians.

Chief O'Brien, weariness personified, sighed deeply and rose from his perch atop a severed tree stump.

"No Cardassians," he reported. The captain grunted in reply. "And the Natives went thataway."

Worf snorted. The last was perfectly obvious without the scan, even to a confirmed non-Native nontracker like Miles Edward O'Brien. Undaunted, the chief continued his scan. On a whim, he turned the probe antenna straight upward and expanded the focus to search right up through the atmosphere. The energy readings flew right off the scale, forcing him to recalibrate.

"Captain, I think I've got something here."

Sisko ambled close, waiting silently until O'Brien could analyze what he was seeing. The energy was utterly unlike the fields of electromagnetic potentia that had earlier blanketed Sierra-Bravo . . . and they'd kicked them all offline anyway, at least in this hemisphere. Instead, the readings looked more like—

"Energy discharges," he concluded. He looked up to find himself the center of attention of four pairs of eyeballs. "Captain, there's a bloody war going on above our heads!"

Sisko frowned, then hissed through his teeth. "A battle? Is the *Defiant* involved?"

"Can't tell with this blasted thing," said O'Brien, frustrated. "Now, if I had access to a ship's sensor screen, I could tell you anything you wanted to know."

"My God," muttered the captain, so softly that O'Brien felt like an eavesdropper. "What is happening? Where is my ship?"

The chief scowled, noticing a faint modulated signal beneath the savage energy discharges. He fiddled with the built-in filters, trying to bring up the subspace transmissions. Listening for a moment, he thought he had caught the drift. "Sir," he said, feeling a nervous flutter, "I just picked out a message about the *Defiant*."

"Well? What's happening?" Sisko shot forth a hand to grip the chief by the shoulder.

"It's . . . mind, I'm not certain of this; it's just an inverted echo inside the general weapons fire. It's not all that clear."

"Spit it out, man!"

O'Brien pursed his lips. "They're saying—something about the *Defiant,* they know it by name, being shot down and . . . crashing into the ocean. Destroyed, they're claiming. Many days ago. But I've known them wrong plenty of times, sir."

Despite the desperate need for military intelligence on the battlefield, the chief suddenly felt awash in guilt for relaying what was really little more than a speculative reconstruction of message fragments. *But what could I do? What the hell could I do?* he demanded, finding no answer but the obvious.

The captain massaged his forehead directly above the bridge of his nose. "Keep monitoring, Chief O'Brien. Alert me to any changes."

* * *

Ensign Wabak sat in the command chair, resisting the temptation to fold his legs up; *too much like a little kid,* he told himself. He forced himself to sit like a Klingon—with knees spread wide, clutching the armrests and scowling at the forward screen.

"Joson," called Ensign Weymouth, her voice quavering. At Wabak's glare, she corrected herself: "Sorry . . . sir, I think you should see this. Picked it up on a short-range scan into the upper atmosphere, about a thousand kilometers orbit."

Wabak sat back, curious as to what was worrying Miss Weymouth now. The lines of force she was projecting onto the viewer made no sense to Wabak at all . . . something in a sensor scan? "Analyze, Ensign," he ordered, praying to the Prophets that he would understand her analysis and not be forced to ask for an explanation of the explanation.

He needn't have worried. "Sir, it's a space battle. The Cardassians are taking a pounding from somebody!"

Abruptly, the cryptic swirls and colored surfaces on the viewer swam into focus as he realized what he was looking at: Weymouth was right; if anything she understated it—the Cardassians were suffering a right royal thumping. Already, three ships were damaged almost beyond repair, and the rest were withdrawing as fast as they could to a high orbit. But the offer was not accepted. The attack continued.

"N'Kduk-Thag," he said, "what the hell is happening up there?"

"It is my belief that the planetary defenses have finally concluded that the Cardassian ships are a threat. They no longer will allow the Cardassians to stay in any altitude orbit. The Cardassians are withdrawing—perhaps we can pick up some of their message traffic."

Wabak sat on the edge of the chair, looking from Ensign Nick to the viewer and back to the utterly unemotional Erd'k'teedak science officer. Nick twisted his head to an impossible angle (for anyone but an Erd'k'teedak). Then at last, he was ready to report.

"Sir, they are leaving orbit. Their ships are already leaving orbit and jumping to warp. They are abandoning whatever Cardassians remain alive on the planet surface. Correction, there has been one beam-aboard."

"A beaming?" demanded Weymouth; "from thirty thousand kilometers?" She sounded incredulous.

"Nick, what about this beam-out? Who, the commander of the group?"

"Negative. Evidently he beamed himself out without help from the Cardassians. They are surprised by his appearance."

There was only one possible explanation. "Hah, he was a Dominion agent, maybe even a changeling!" Wabak sat back, smirking. "My friends, I have just realized we're going to win this stupid war."

"We are?" asked Weymouth. "How can you be so sure?"

"Because, Ensign, no matter how much we may distrust the Klingons or even the Romulans, we're nowhere near the point of sending *spies* into our allies' ranks." Wabak wiped the grin from his face, struggling for sternness once more. "But what about the Gul-in-charge? What's happened to him?"

For a long moment Ensign Nick did not appear to notice the question, but Wabak knew he was waiting until he had positively located the precise element of the traffic that would detail the GIC's fate. After a solid minute, Nick turned to face Wabak, seated in a chair that was becoming altogether too comfortable. "The Gul-in-charge has vanished, and none of the attackers seem particularly concerned that they're leaving him behind with the rest of the soldiers."

"Ditching him? Yet another reason we're going to win."

"They do not appear to like Gul Ragat very much." said Ensign Nick as sort of a summary appendix. "There is no sadness nor concern as to his fate. Sir, the last of the Cardassian ships has left orbit. Whoever is left on the surface is on his own now."

Wabak couldn't resist another face-splitting smile. "Perfect, Nick. Just the sort of odds I like."

CHAPTER
11

DR. BASHIR LEANED BACK against the brine-dark canyon cliff, wishing the throbbing in his leg would cease, cursing the chap who invented the alleged analgesic in the hypospray, struggling not to frighten Dax by letting his inner grimace appear on his face, wondering how many charges were left in his Cardassian disruptor—and ignoring, as best he could, the savage, overpowering urge to cough . . . the early symptom of a very serious case of cyanogen poisoning, a small prelude of what was to come and a only tiny morsel of what the members of the away team must already be suffering.

Ten meters downstream in the canyon, Dax lost a similar struggle. She began to cough, and it turned into a choking match that left her out of breath and red-faced. She regained her composure after a battle. But even from where he sat, unable to move because every shift sent a spasm of agony through his splinted femur, Bashir could see the trickle of blood down Dax's chin. The deadly, atmospheric toxins were taking their toll. *And there's not a damned thing I can do about it. Isn't modern medicine wonderful?*

"They're coming," said Dax, her voice hoarse, nearly a whisper. She held up a hand with fingers spread wide. "Five minutes. Ready. Wait for my order."

Bashir nodded, not trusting even his own enhanced will enough to speak aloud. He practiced extending his gun hand a few times, seeing if he still had the mobility and stability to shoot without burning the lovely Jadzia by accident. He realized to his amusement that he could take advantage of his infirmity: he could rest the muzzle of the disruptor against his splint to create a stable gun platform. Dry-lipped, he sweltered and waited.

The latinum-tinged soil of the canyon floor reflected the sunlight and intensified the heat—*which gives the Cardassians rather the edge,* he thought in grim resignation. Bashir, despite being raised in the desert, felt sweat beading on his forehead. The moisture would not evaporate; the humidity was much too high for such a blessing.

This planet has the most insane weather patterns I can remember. The wild mood swings from cold to hot, dry to humid, high to low pressure reminded him of nothing so much as the myriad subcultures of the Natives, an anarchy of opposites. As Dax described them, the Tiffnaki, or whatever they called themselves now, were open-handed and generous, pacifistic, full of enthusiasm. But the aged Gul Ragat had spoken bitterly of black-hearted, vicious predator-villages, full of bloodthirsty Natives, that might have inspired Bram Stoker and other vampire writers of the Victorian Age.

The five minutes passed as one. Dax silently counted them down with her fingers, but each seemed only a few seconds long. Bashir's sensitive ears began to hear the high-pitched yawn of Cardassian skimmers and the scrape of metal-shod boots on the rocky floor. He trained his disruptor on the agreed-upon target: a shatter of broken granite at the top of a narrow defile. Dax, presumably, aimed at another a few meters farther on.

The first Cardassian scouts peeped into view. If they were using infrared, Bashir understood, he and Dax would be sitting ducks. But they relied upon the Cardassians' observed arrogance and evident disdain for their primative, ignorant enemies. The scouts rolled along, riding their skimmers with lazy ease, perfect indifference.

"Julian," warned Dax. "Now!"

The doctor reacted as one would expect from his enhanced muscles and nerve clusters. But even so, Dax beat him to the punch. The pair fired into the respective shattered tops of the canyon walls.

At first, the Caradassians stopped, staring in every direction with suspicion and betrayal. Disruptors! The troops were being attacked in the field by their own men! It took some seconds for the confusion to clear and for the Cardassians to begin returning fire.

But the damage to the cliff face was irreparable and catastrophic.

With a scream like dive-bombing harpies, the rocks tore themselves loose from the wall, caterwauling downhill and crashing into a heap directly athwart the Cardassians' attack. As a low rumble shook the ground, the doctor's leg jerked off the rock it was balanced on and thudded to the ground. An icepick rammed into his thigh, or so it felt. He dropped the disruptor pistol and leaned over to clutch at his splinted bone, tears dotting his eyes from the relentless pain. But after a few moments, the main bunch of Cardassians, trapped by the pair of avalanches, retreated to plink over the rocks toward Dax's and Bashir's position. The skimmers, of course, moved along smartly, rising up over the rockfall and swooping forward.

If they weren't using sensors before, they surely are now, thought Bashir. He abandoned all hope of remaining unknown . . . as he had long ago accepted with equanamity that he would someday die—and what difference would that make to the world? He was not afraid of what would happen to him in the battle. This made him a deadly opponent indeed.

Quickly thumbing the disruptor down the scale to heavy stun, Bashir began to shoot the skimmers out of the sky. Dax was no match for his synthesized aim and manufactured speed; it was as easy as beating Chief O'Brien at darts. She herself only managed one hit, and that against an already stunned Cardassian in a skimmer that settling gently to ground, the pilot having ceased giving orders.

When the last flying Cardassian had been blown out of the sky, Dax struggled to her feet and crept closer to the fallen bodies. *She's making sure they're not feigning unconsciousness,* he concluded. It was a wise precaution, but unnecessary: Bashir knew what he had bagged.

She pulled the transponder-pack from each cycle, preventing the bulk of the Cardassian regiment from calling the skimmers back. Then the commander scurried back to the relative safety of the tiny natural caves, pursued by disruptor blasts. *"Oooh* rah!" she exclaimed, pumping her fist in the air. "Mission finished. We've got 'em boxed in for half a day at least. When it gets intolerable, we'll hijack one of those skimmers and get the hell out of here."

The estimate proved optimistic. The Cardassians had no sooner parsed the loss of their skimmer-scouts but they decided they needed intelligence—*which Dax should have predicted,* thought Bashir, *considering what we all know about the Obsidian Order and the Cardassian obsession with spycraft.* Bashir had, in fact, predicted the attempt. He whispered to Commander Dax: "Jadzia, they're going to try to penetrate at both ends of the rockfall simultaneously. They're also going to set some soldiers scaling the walls of the canyon to drop on us from above." The skimmer was always an option, but as long as they could keep the Cardassians pinned, Bashir was as reluctant as Dax to flee the scene.

She nodded.

Bashir was wrong on one count, as it happened: the Cardassians tried only one breakout around the rockpile, not both ends, as the doctor himself would have done. Bashir and Dax waited until the luckless vanguard was across the artificial ridge and part-way down before dropping them under heavy stun, so they would roll onto the Federation side of the avalanche. If they fell back among their comrades, they could be revived by a cortical stimulator.

Bashir began to drag himself forward to make sure they hadn't sustained injury rolling down the jagged rocks. But Dax held him back. "Julian, don't." Her face was pinched, taut with suppressed emotion.

"Jadzia, I'm a doctor. I have to tend the wounded."

She shook her head. "Not during combat . . . not when we have no facility for stashing prisoners."

Dax again got ahold of the tricorder. "I'm picking up a sensor echo of *about* half a dozen Cardassians skulking along the rim of the canyon."

"About?"

She shrugged. "The minerals in the cliff face blocks a precise scan." The doctor swallowed and readied his stolen disruptor.

Nine soldiers dropped into the ravine, relying on their natural Cardassian strength to land safely after a twelve-meter fall. They hit the ground on their feet but were momentarily stunned. Moments later, they were thoroughly stunned.

"Now," said Bashir, "they will parlay." Dax nodded, agreeing with the assessment.

Five minutes of silence elapsed while they waited to see who would win. At last, a magnified voice called across the rock wall—in Federation Standard.

"Commander Dax, how nice to discover you have survived the crash of your ship. And the doctor, too! We are quite overjoyed at such good fortune."

Dax poked at her tricorder for a moment. It was a simple trick to modify it into a bullhorn; *even I could do it,* he thought, *little though I know about communications circuitry.* But when she began to speak, it wasn't her own voice, but a booming, Godlike presence that rattled the remaining precariously balanced stones high above and echoed around the skull. "Cardassian prisoners, you will be treated well in a Federation war-prisoner colony. Do not fear for your lives. What you have been told about the Federation is a lie."

The Cardassian voice laughed, a spritely elf. "Oh, come now, Commander! Do you not think we have scanned you and know there are but two, yourself and Doctor Bashir? We also know there is a mob of aborigines approaching with pitchforks and useless nonworking Native technology, and we are prepared to deal with them swiftly. Do not expect rescue."

"And do *you* not think," said Dax with a grin, "that *we* don't know that your ships are gone, you have no reinforcements, and you have been abandoned to your fate by your cowardly comrades?" She monkeyed with the tricorder again. "Surrender," she concluded in her normal voice, "is your only option."

Bashir lowered his thick, black brows, puzzled. *How does she know the Cardassian ships have left?* After a moment's thought, the answer leaped into his brain. *Obviously, if their ships were still here, they could have been beamed from the canyon right into our laps!* Ergo, they were alone, abandoned, completely cut off.

After a long pause, the Cardassian voice resumed, now assuming a tone of let's-all-get-together-for-our-own-good. *Cardassians are so predictable,* thought the doctor.

"We appear to be in the same phalanx, Commander. We are indeed marooned, as you have deduced. And you are two of how many survivors, stranded alone so very far from your Federation home? I wonder which of our respective governments will return the quickest?"

Bashir smiled, reaching for the tricorder. After a moment's raised eyebrow, Dax surrendered it to him. Bashir had his own deductions with which to impress the Cardassian, who was most likely nothing more than a lieutenant, one rank above high sergeant. "My good friend," he said, "I think we both know just how long it will be before a *Cardassian* ship comes to the rescue of Gul Ragat the Banished. Renegades, masterless men—who cares whether you live or die?"

Bashir could almost hear the sigh in the Cardassian centurion's voice. "Well, it appears you know as much about us as we know about you. A pity we seem unable to stand shoulder-to-shoulder and face this harsh environment together—which may well turn out to be our home for the rest of our lives. Which may not be too long. You are aware of the cyanogens?"

Bashir said nothing, and the centurion continued. "But of course you are, Dr. Bashir. However, we have something you do not, I suspect. We have a

complete chemical roadmap for scrubbing the cyanogens from the food supply, using only native animal life. If we can solve the long-term food problem,
Doctor, then together we can carve a life here."

Dax took the tricorder megaphone back from
Bashir. "But you are forgetting . . . that unlike you,
we aren't renegades. The Federation knows where
we are, and they *will* come looking for us. In fact, I'd
venture to bet there will be a Federation ship on the
ground here in just a day or two." She smiled and
winked at Bashir.

"So there is another alternative to stumbling
around until we cough ourselves to death," she
concluded. "You will surrender. You will throw your
weapons over the rocks and we will destroy them.
Walk out with your hands on your heads, fingers
interlaced—and we will put in a good word for you
when the ship arrives."

"Ho! Then it appears," said the mystery voice,
"that we have reached an impasse. Commander,
Doctor, a good day to you both. Let's see who will
crack first, and whether you choke on your own
blood before that wonderful starship arrives!" Then
both sides fell silent.

"They're going to launch one more attack," said
Bashir; Dax nodded agreement. "And then, perhaps,
they may talk settlement . . . *if* we can convince
them that a Federation ship is really here." *If we can
get word via radio that we need the Defiant. If she's
ready to fly. If we're willing to chance the planetary
defense screen to intimidate a couple of hundred
Cardassian troopers. If she's not shot down halfway
from the ocean to here—if, if, if!*

"The Natives are only a few hours away," said Dax, studying her tricorder readings. "And I'm sure they know there's an enemy here and intend to engage, for they haven't deviated from their straight-line course since I first spotted them." She smiled, sending all sorts of inappropriate feelings flooding through the good Doctor Julian Bashir. "Just keep your fingers crossed that the Cardassians don't decide to turn Klingon on us and launch an all-out assault to break out."

He grunted in pain. It was nothing Dax had said . . . just the analgesic wearing off.

Per the captain's instructions, Constable Odo flew high overhead playing "native hawk," keeping a topside view of the Native troops as they roved into battle. *Natives . . ridiculous name. So typical of Commander Dax to peg the natives with such a cognomen, lapped up with eager mirth by the away team. And then she disappears from orbit into the depths of the ocean without so much as—*

Odo cut the dreadful thought off at the pass. The last thing in Sierra-Bravo he wanted to think about was the rumored demise of Jadzia Dax, everyone's exasperating favorite. Her death, or Jadzia's death anyway, would come soon enough; it did for all solids. The captain would die, Doctor Bashir, Garak, Quark . . . *well, every dark cloud has its latinum lining.* They would all die, everyone Odo had ever known. But he would still live on, alone and friendless. Even Major Kira would—

"No!" With a wrenching effort, the constable forced his attention back to the ragged but steady progress made by the native prodigies across the trackless, roadless terrain. They had hastily thrown together a dozen rattletrap *jalopies* (to use an old Earth term Odo had picked up from centuries-old police blotters), and were puttering their way at forty kilometers per hour toward a rendezvous with the largest Cardassian force so far encountered. Chief O'Brien's tricorder readings pinpointed the enemy, and Colonel-Mayor Asta-ha was on fire to lead the charge personally. So Odo flew overhead to make sure the Natives' newly invented "strategic military imposture" didn't degenerate into an attempt to herd cats.

Is she alive? Is she dead? Is there a ship to take us home, or are we stranded here until somebody in the Federation, remembers to go looking for us? And will that be before or after everyone but me dies of cynaogen poisoning? Try as he might, Odo couldn't keep his brain from returning to the overwhelming question: was Dax alive or smashed to small bits in the wreck of the *Defiant?*

The hardest part, if the worst were true, would not be the grief and loss of losing a friend, nor even the impossible task of replacing Dax. It would be *explaining to Nerys* how he—Odo—had allowed her to die on his watch. That thought was frightening enough to make him momentarily lose his shape.

Flapping far overhead, Odo made a number of modifications to his basic bird body—adding telescoping eyes, increasing his overall length for better gliding, and bumping up wingspan-to-mass ratio by thinning his wings.

He peered below and zoomed in on various jalopies, packed to their ragtop roofs with a snowballing
mob of Natives. With the power grid down and the
Natives thrown upon their own resources, they had
progressed so remarkably that the constable was
frightened. Small clusters of Natives—under the
ultimate direction of Owena-da and a new recruit,
Ang-Nak Pungent Halflife Potato-Eater (the universal translator was having a field day)—were developing new secret weapons, even as the column crawled
across the brittle living carpet of Sierra-Bravo fern.
The carpet flared and scuttled out of the way as best
it could (several of the plant species on Sierra-Bravo
had developed mobility, the ability to step up out of
the soil and march away to better times and climes).

Odo zoomed in to fifty power but was still unable
to pierce the veil of secrecy surrounding the Natives'
work. Having discussed with Worf a grand treatise
from the last century on "black ops," the one by
Snorri Thwackum, the Natives had gone crazy for
secret projects, intelligence gathering, and encryption. The upshot was that nobody on the away team,
not even the captain himself, knew what the Natives
would unleash upon their enemies. Still, Odo knew
his duty. He panned and zoomed and tried for
different angles, hoping that one of them had made a
mistake. None ever did, of course.

The constable gave it up and decided instead to go
high and higher, searching out the enemy to warn
Captain Sisko—who, along with the rest of the
team, was staying nearly a full kilometer back of the
massed might of the colonel-mayor. Odo pumped

his mighty wings, grabbing air and propelling himself so high that had he needed to breathe, he would have been in serious trouble.

At this height, Odo again shifted his shape, voluminously expanding the wingspan and adding a natural pair of slats to extend and thicken the wings as necessary. He trained his eyes on a distant defile, so far below that even with the maximum magnification his eyes would allow (he had copied them from the *Vib Sokorath* of the Claudius colony) he still could barely make out anything with a "footprint" smaller than four square meters.

But as he flapped his way closer, Constable Odo saw what he had anticipated with simultaneous eagerness and dread: an entire two-hundred-soldier battalion of the last remaining Cardassians, now stranded, as their ships had left, and without their MIA leader, the local Gul. Dipping low, Odo saw that they had been stopped by a recent rockslide. . . . Sabotage? But there was no army on the other side of the rockwall.

It would take the Native "cavalry" less than an hour to make contact with the enemy. *And then we'll see how useful these so-called Doomsday weapons really are.*

Odo made a careful count, spied what he could of the Cardassian weaponry, and discovered several rows of dead or unconscious Cardassians on the other side of the rockslide, laid neatly into rows and columns by a considerate but invisible enemy. And then, on his third and final pass through the canyon, Constable Odo caught one last piece of intel that by itself would have made up for everything else being lost. On Odo's last pass below the cliffs that defined the defile, he caught sight of two evident Natives. And then, upon higher magnification, he realized that the pair were not natives, but two people that the constable knew well: Julian Bashir and Jadzia Dax! The former had his leg in a splint, but otherwise the two were unhurt.

Wheeling about at breathtaking Gs (had he had any breath to take), Odo flashed away. For once in his life, he got to play bearer of *good* news. Dax was alive, Dax and Bashir! It would be cause for celebration among the oft unseemly and overly emotional "solids" of the away team. Even Constable Odo allowed himself a short moment of delicious relief.

But all the emotionalism rather begged the main question, which the constable had been asking himself ever since seeing the two: how in the world did Dax and the doctor *get off* a crashing starship? Odo snorted, recognizing it was going to be a long, long time before he prised any answers out of those two.

CHAPTER
12

KAI WINN stood utterly still, rooted to her spot in Operations, staring at the dark stains on the floor where her protege had been assaulted. Standing still and silent, she thought, had been the hardest thing she had ever had to do in a lifetime of hardship. Winn hadn't realized until that moment just how much Kira Nerys meant to her . . . and to Bajor.

She is the new Bajor, thought the Kai. *I am not the future, I am the past. Nerys is the future. If she dies, Bajor dies.* Winn had no idea what Kira's connection to the planet and the Prophets was, but she knew it was real and deep.

When at last the Kai could swallow without gagging and speak without screaming, when she had mastered herself, she glided across Ops and sat down in a chair by the science console. She could not keep all of the disgust out of her face, but that was all right: the dean would expect a certain loathing after she witnessed the punishment.

The dean began to speak. "When the prisoner brings the far-seeing anomaly—"

"Don't talk to me," said the Kai.

"You will demonstrate its use to—"

"Don't talk to me." The force of her simple imperative so caught the dean by surprise that he fell silent.

Kai Winn closed her eyes, feeling in need of spiritual and physical cleansing . . . prayer and a bath. She blinked once, twice—

THIRTY YEARS AGO

—shaken awake by the emotionless sergeant to see her Gul standing over her, his gray face positively ashen. "By your own Prophets," whispered Gul Ragat huskily, "what have you done?"

"My lord?"

"I . . . did you. . . ." Ceasing his futile attempt to find words, Ragat handed Sister Winn an order pad. Dizzy and confused, she sat up inside the cold tent, took the pad, and touched the Cardassian logo in its center.

The grisly visage of Legate Migar faded into existence in the center of the pad. He spoke in Cardassian, but Winn, who had the gift, spoke the language as well as the young Gul. "Gul Ragat, you will return instantly via transporter from the General Lyll Military Academy in North Riis. This morning, one of my guards was discovered drunk on duty.

He has been disciplined. But before the punishment was administered, the traitorous wretch attempted to mitigate his sentence by telling us all a story about a certain young priestess.

"Mr. Kulakat told us that on the day of the bulletin tea he was walking his rounds near the alpha code room. He heard a strange noise and went to investigate. He found the door to the code room itself unlocked and unlatched, still open a crack. He found a Bajoran priestess in front of the door, where she told him she had, and I quote, 'pushed it open and looked inside.'" Migar frowned grimly on the recorded message. "That priestess was your servant Winn. She is now considered an enemy of the state and is wanted for questioning as a hostile witness. You have three hours, Gul Ragat."

The message ended, and Sister Winn handed the pad back to her own Gul. She sat with resignation, waiting for the Prophets to speak into her ear again, as they had when the lustful corporal had threatened her. *What do I do? How do I get the holocam to the Resistance? How do I live? What do I do?* But nothing came to Winn, not even a whisper. She was alone.

"Get up," said a voice from behind the Gul. Winn recognized it, but she bent to look around Ragat anyway. Neemak Counselor was grinning, staring to the left side of the priestess, and rubbing his hands as if washing them. "M'Lord Gul Ragat, I should be delighted to escort this prisoner back to the legate's headquarters. If you will permit?"

"No," said Gul Ragat.

"Then I will happy to . . . what the hell do you mean, No?" Neemak stared beligerently at Ragat.

He would never speak that way to a Gul unless he knew that Ragat was on his way out and down, thought Winn.

"I mean *No,*" said the Gul, insisting. "She is mine. She has been with me for many years, serving loyally not only me but my father as well, before he died. I, not you, will take her to Legate Migar's villa."

Neemak glowered. At last, the counselor executed a perfect and grace-filled bow that nevertheless spoke eloquently of his contempt and detestation of his nominal master. There had been persistent rumors, and Sister Winn knew them as well as any. *They say Ragat's uncle is the true head of the Obsidian order,* she remembered, *and the other Guls have resented Ragat his whole life for it.* Whether he became a political pawn in the struggle between the Cardassian regular army—under Gul Dukat—and the spymasters, Gul Ragat's career had just ended. Never again would he be trusted, invited to the bulletin tea, never would he have the ear of a legate or a Gul as powerful as Dukat. By allowing his servant—his *priestess*—to dare so much, peeking into the holiest of Obsidian Order holies, the almighty *code room,* even if they never discovered her true treachery, Ragat had proven himself an embarrassment to his father and a disgrace to his house and the Empire. *He will pay, by the Prophets, will he be made to pay.*

And of course, she also knew that they would discover her ultimate treachery . . . for they would question her. Gul Dukat himself would question her—and when he was finished, there would be no "her" left to hold a secret. Not even a secret that was a certain death sentence. In fact, the Cardassians could be so unpleasant that she might scream out her confession early to stop the pain and end it all.

But for the moment, there was no reason for Gul Ragat to know anything. So when he crouched down, looked Winn in the eye, and said, "Tell me what happened, Sister Winn," she looked him right back and lied through her teeth.

"The door was open, my lord, and I did look inside. I was curious. I didn't even know what the room was . . . I didn't know it was a code room! There was no sign on the door, for the sake of the Prophets." She allowed a single tear to roll down her cheek. It dropped to the floor of the tent and made a tiny stain.

Gul Ragat sighed deeply and shook his head. "Oh Winn, Winn, Winn. What can I do with you?" He appeared truly upset, saddened, in pain. *But would he feel a thing if I were an anonymous Bajoran he didn't know? I doubt it.*

"My lord, I know what is going to happen. I know what they must do to me. My life will be forfeit——"

"Winn! It should never come to that, if you're innocent of any mal intent."

She smiled wanly. "I will be given to Gul Dukat, for he is the expert in these sorts of things. In his zeal to drag out of me secrets I don't possess, he will become over-enthusiastic. My Lord Gul, I'm not as young as I look, and I'm not in the best of health. My heart. I doubt I shall survive." Winn looked up at the young man—boy rather—who was pathetically convinced that she had served him loyally for years. There was, in fact, nothing whatever wrong with her heart (that she knew of!). "Lord, I wish only to serve you myself on this final journey. You are . . . a good man, Gul Ragat."

Playing the scene for all it was worth, Sister Winn lowered her head as if shamed. Queerly, she *felt* shame—illusory, but nonetheless painful. "I know how you feel about us. I know you have high hopes for Bajor's ultimate progress into full citizenship within the Empire."

Neemak couldn't help snorting in amused disbelief, but whether at Ragat's peculiar beliefs about the future of Bajor or at Winn's preposterous loyalty to the Gul, who would be sending her to certain, painful death, she could not determine. "I'll listen to no more of this," said the counselor with a sneer. "I, at least, have work to do for the Empire."

Winn and Ragat shared a glance. Both knew what that work was: Neemak Counselor reported back to some superior somewhere all that he saw and heard in the Gul's household, and right now the oily snitch—who could never meet a gaze full on—was scurrying off like a roach to do just that.

"Let me dress and prepare you, my lord," she said when Neemak slapped the tent flap aside and stomped away. "Let me have that one last honor."

Gul Ragat closed his eyes as if fatigued. He shook his head, but then nodded. "Fetch my breastplate then, and my First Class jacket, gloves, and knife."

Winn nodded in resignation. "The baton," she added, "and the field pack. Your sash and ribbons of honor."

"Yes, everything." He smiled with an attempt at ruefulness. "Indeed, you are not the only one to fear the meeting with the legate. Migar will have my head for breakfast."

You arrogant, self-blinded egotist! she accused. *Do you really compare your* career setback *with the torture and murder of your favorite Bajoran slave? Prophets save your soul, for no one else seems to care a whit about it, especially not you.*

Ragat waved the guards away when they tried to take her elbows. He shook his head, shooing them back to the rest of the camp. "Make ready," he said. "I shall need an honor guard after we reach the academy."

They returned to the observation post where the Gul had left his pack, where Sister Winn had left her vital holocam. There was no trick to retrieving it: She picked up the pack, the gul turned his back, she removed the camera and restored it to her sleeve, and then put the pack on Gul Ragat's back. The autostraps locked into place. Simplicity itself, with no one watching.

All right. Now what? There was no answer. But one virtue Sister Winn had learned, over many laborious years of Cardassian occupation, was the ability to wait endlessly for her moment.

Despite outward resignation, Winn plotted furiously. The path to the General Lyll Military Academy was not long, skirting the floating section of Riis and winding basically northward, through the Street of Many-Voiced Vegetables (called "the Voice" by the residents), passing close on the Blue Order Lodge, the old farmers' exchange, three temples to the Prophets, the historic Barak Nai House (home of the First Minister of two centuries past), and the

Hall of the Legion of Prophets (where Barada Vai had been sent, in Winn's elaborate ruse, to get him away from the putative bombing that never occurred), before at last crossing the Swifts—a spur that looped off the Shakiristi River and rejoined it after sliding over a waterfall—and leading to the Academy.

General Lyll had led a small expeditionary force against a group of Anti-Prophets seventy-eight years ago. His victory was elusive and ambiguous, but he either had a patron in the prefecture council or else a good PR man, for he ended up eponym to a military academy and several public squares. The Cardassians, in a show of "respect" for their conquered victims, had kept the old name while expelling all Bajorans and taking over the school for the scions of Cardassian captains, admirals, and generals. They installed transporters, mindful of the crowded schedules of dignitaries who needed to give commencement speeches . . . thus, it was the nearest Cardassian facility whence to transport back to Legate Migar's compound.

Growing desperate, Winn visualized each of the major buildings en route to the Academy: they were generally small—Bajorans did not need palaces or fortresses, unlike the Cardassians—and surrounded by open spaces filled with innocent civilians who would surely be hurt or killed as Winn broke for freedom and her guards opened fire. So intent was she that she didn't even notice when the Gul, his prisoner, and his honor guard actually set out, and her brain was so filled with imagined escapes that she had no room to be afraid.

She shuffled along the cobbled street called "the Voice," seeing not where she was but where she would be in a few minutes. More and more, it appeared that she would have to make her break in the midst of a mob, and trust to the Prophets that no innocents were cut down by disruptor blasts. *If it were only my own life, I would willingly sacrifice it rather than put others at risk,* she told herself. *But the holos are vital to the Resistance; they must survive!* She wondered whether it were true or just a damn good rationalization for cowardice.

She hesitated at the first temple, a fine affair with colored-light murals, cushioned benches, and a laquered cabinet to hold the sacred texts. Winn attended services there the last time she was in Riis, as a recent graduate of Seminary. But something crouching inside her stomach warned her that the High Temple was not the place for her final act of worship. Just as she resumed walking again, the impatient sergeant behind her shoved her forward.

Taking advantage of the momentum, Sister Winn hurried to Gul Ragat's side. "My lord," she said, trying for hopeful anxiety, an easy emotion to project, "the next temple is a particular favorite of ours. It is rude and classless, but not without charm. It was erected a thousand years ago by Kilikarri, the Emissary to the Prophets, after he founded Riis on the Shakiristi River where he had cast his net and caught exactly one hundred fish and the third Scroll of Prophecy."

Ragat said nothing, trudging onward, his gaze fixed forward on his crumbling future. But Winn thought he turned his head slightly, stretching his ears to what might be the last request she would make of him.

"My lord, I should like to spend a moment worshipping in the Temple of Kilikarri before we continue over the river."

Rather than answer her directly, Gul Ragat turned to his Captain of Foot. "Major Duko, what is the time?"

"It is thirteen minutes past the thirteenth hour, Gul Ragat," said the laconic major.

"My priestess has been with me for a long time, Major. We shall stop and refresh ourselves for five minutes at the Temple of Kilikarri."

"As you command, sir."

They passed the Blue Order Lodge, a square, solid, four-storey house done all in shades of blue. It lay open, as it always did to members of the journalistic order, but there was hardly anybody present at midday, the members mostly being at work. Just past the Lodge, Winn saw the unprepossessing wooden temple, only one storey tall with neither door in the doorframe nor glass in the windows.

The procession paused beside the wooden colonnade, Gul Ragat still not looking directly at Winn. But the wary eyes of the sergeant and his crew followed her intently as she stepped laboriously down the short stairway, careful not to slip and fall, her ample flesh working against her. Struck by an inspiration from the Prophets, though not yet aware of what They planned, Winn stopped at the bottom, clutched her chest with one hand and clung for dear life to the railing with the other. "Ohhh . . ." she breathed, feeling her face go white—either a magnificent acting job she didn't know was in her, or else the hand of the divine.

"Winn," said Ragat, shocked out of his aloofness, "are you all right?"

"I'll—be all right—in a—moment, my lord." She sat on the bottom step to recover from the nonexistent heart seizure. Then she stood, grim-visaged, and marched resolutely into the temple. The Cardassian guards followed her, not allowing Winn to vanish from their sight for even a heartbeat. She buried her hands in her sleeve-pockets and took hold of the holocam, she knew not why.

She had never been inside the Kilikarri before. The interior of the temple was warm and soft, the umber-stained woods polished to a sheen, the benches unpadded but oddly comforting to the eye. As she walked down the center aisle, she could not help thinking, *this may be the last temple I see . . . this could be the last time I bow to the Prophets . . . this might be my last glimpse of the sacred texts.* The thoughts were not only unworthy of a vessel of the Prophets, they interfered with scheming a way out.

An old man was walking up and out as Winn trudged down and in. He was gnarled and bent, so that he looked at the ground as he placed his sandaled feet carefully, lest he lose his footing. He didn't see her and walked right into Winn's midsection.

She could have stepped out of the way—when the priestess wished, she could be remarkably agile, as she had proven at the long-ago bulletin tea that started all the nonsense. But a whisper at the back of her mind told her to let the old man bump her.

"Clumsy Bajoran cattle!" she snarled—in Cardassian. The man smelled strongly of fish . . . *as Kilikarri did?* she wondered.

Even her own guards were taken aback. She heard one of them gasp. The old man stopped cold, not moving, waiting, with a serenity Winn could only dream about, for whatever the Prophets had in store for him that afternoon.

Sister Winn savagely yanked her hands out of the sleeves, grabbed the bent, old man's belt, and rudely shoved him out of her way. Her fingers were never surer. She found his coin purse, prised it open with two digits, and dropped the holocam in it from her palm. It could have hit the lip of the purse and clattered onto the floor, but it slipped in noiselessly.

The ancient could have cried out when he felt the sudden weight, but he said nothing. The guards might have seen . . . but the first one was blocked by Winn's body, and the second was screened by the first. She could not close the purse in the instant she had, but no one chose to look inside. The shriveled fisherman groveled until she was past, then he resumed his ancient footsteps past the sergeant and out. *A minute after he passes, not a single soul will remember he ever lived—except me.*

Winn bowed, made the opening salutations to Those, and prayed as she never had before. She prayed for wisdom—not her own, for she needed only boldness, but for the ancient fisher prince, that he might recognize what she had slipped into his pouch and understand its import . . . and that he might be old enough, yet not too old—old enough to remember Bajor before the Occupation, but not too old to remember how to contact the Riis cell.

When she had said all the prayers she thought the Prophets could stand to hear at one sitting, she rose, exited the temple with bowed head and lethargic step, and rejoined the parade. Gul Ragat nodded, and they recommenced their stately, measured tread toward the crescent-moon bridge across the Swifts and the last, upward slope to the redstone walls of the General Lyll Military Academy.

CHAPTER
13

JADZIA DAX eyed the rock wall uneasily. Something was wrong. She could feel it—somewhere. *Some slight noise, below conscious hearing? A nagging, illogical doubt.*

The knife-pain in her lungs twinged sharply. The pain was almost constant—the cyanogens in the air, Dax knew—and the only reason she wouldn't cry out was that she knew the doctor was suffering as much and more.

Behind her, several meters away, lay the charming Julian Bashir. He preferred the solitude, since his pain-killer had worn off, and he couldn't quite hide the agony of his broken and engineer-mended femur. Dax hunched over, gripping her knees in a desperate hug. She felt guilty beyond belief: *I was in command—the crash wasn't my fault, but it's my responsibility! I did the best I could doctoring the doc.*

But my best wasn't good enough. My crewman, my friend, is suffering, and I damn well take it hard.

She choked down her urge to scuttle across and hover solicitously over Bashir. But she wouldn't allow her own insecurities to strip the man of his dignity. As a doctor and Starfleet officer, he wouldn't see eyeball to eyeball with Dax's stubborn interpretation of command responsibility. But she had every right to hold herself accountable, nobody was going to take it away from her.

Her stomach had begun to ache, and her joints, and she felt dizzy . . . in fact, she was exhibiting every symptom Bashir had told her she would feel (and every other symptom she had imagined) as the cyanogens slowly, inexorably destroyed her body's cellular structure. And there would be a point of no return, after which treatment could slow but not stop her final death. She had no idea how close she was to that point, if indeed she hadn't already crossed it. But at the moment there was nothing she could do about the situation, and she had other fish to scale.

Wait, this time I heard—I thought I heard. . . . She closed her eyes and tilted her head, *almost* hearing a faint scrape at the base of the rockpile. Dax listened intently, crawling right up to the base of the slide and leaning against the dark, raw split of stone broken off by the disruptor beam. The razor-sharp shards of crystal sliced her palm, but she didn't even notice until her hand slipped in the leaking blood.

Dax pressed her ear against the stone, and she heard, sure enough, a regular grinding noise, the sound of Worf sharpening his *d'k tahg* blade against an old-fashioned grinding wheel. *Or the sound of.* . . .

Bashir groaned. Before she could even think, she whispered, "Quiet!" The grinding stopped. But it had been a grinding like—

Dax leapt to her feet. "Julian, get the hell out of here . . . they just drilled a hole in the rocks and they're probably planting an explosive device!"

Wincing, the doctor pulled himself to a kneeling position, his splinted leg sticking out in front of him. Dax crossed the distance in two long-legged strides, grabbed Bashir under the arms, and jerked him onto his one good foot. "Go that way—*now.* I've got something to do!"

"Jadzia," gasped Bashir, "the prisoners. . . ." But she was already gone, for that had been her second thought as well.

The two of them had sent eleven Cardassians into the Land of Nod. Dax pelted to the "boneyard," as she had taken to calling the spot where they'd lain the sleeping souls, and skipped to a halt. She was very big for a woman, but the Drek'la troops were a hell of a lot bigger, and they wore battle armor. *There's no way I can take more than one at a time,* she concluded, with a detached rationality that surprised her, even after seven lifetimes. *Oh well, war is hell.*

She grabbed the nearest snoring soldier, slid him across her shoulders in a paramedic's carry, and tottered off after Bashir. She had not gotten more than twenty meters when the sky fell on her, the earth rose up to kick her in the jaw, and the catacombs of the dead opened beneath her.

By the time she got oriented again (*ground is down, sky is up, canyon walls are*—), the ringing in her ears had subsided enough that she could barely hear the screams behind her. She vaguely remembered toting a Cardassian somewhere for some reason, but he was gone. Turning to look behind her, a wave of dizziness knocked her to the ground again. But she saw the most peculiar sight: the rock wall, which she had reckoned would have blown inward on top of Bashir and herself, was instead kicked *backward,* dumping across the first few rows of legionaires. *Why? Did their sappers screw up?*

An instant later, Dax's questions were answered, as a flaming ball arced across the sky, a miniature sun passing from dawn to dusk in six seconds. When it struck, long past the Drek'la soldiers, it exploded with fury, gouging a three-meter crater in the canyon floor and propelling dozens of Drek'la forward into the remnants of rockfall. It also wrecked the skimmers—their only means of escape from the bombardment. For an instant, she almost forgot the tearing pain in her lungs, so awed was she by the power of the ancient, primitive weapon.

"Julian!" she shouted, "look at that!" She winced when she realized the absurdity of her command. As if he could hear her over the tumult—as if he'd been looking anywhere else!

The world turned upside down. The fireball was followed by a dozen more, and Dax scuttled crablike backwards to Bashir, almost running over his bum leg in her haste. The pair cringed back against the rough granite wall of the defile. Dax plugged her ears with her thumbs while desperately trying to shield her eyes from the steady rain of dust shaken loose above her by the concussions. The dust was filled with sharp grains of latinum that could easily scratch a cornea if they got underneath an eyelid.

The Drek'la soldiers hadn't stayed shell-shocked for long. Their Cardassian lieutenant shouted them into some semblance of cover beneath the landslide that Dax and Bashir had caused so long before. And after a few moments, whoever was lobbing balls of fire either got tired of the game or else ran out of ammunition.

Heads began to peep over the edge of the cliffs twelve meters above. Hooded faces stared down into the canyon . . . and the quick-witted lieutenant bellowed the order to fire. One Native dropped screaming to the canyon floor, dead before striking ground. Instinctively, Dax grabbed for her tricorder before realizing it was gone, left behind somewhere during the confusion of the sudden battle. *Damn, have to be sure to remember to retrieve it.* Memories of Starfleet Academy and the infamous Iotian catastrophe washed her brain.

She cautiously removed her thumbs from her ears, as the explosions had stopped. But then, without warning, the most horrific racket kicked up from the bluffs above, loud enough that she yelped and clapped her full palms over her ears, scrunching up even smaller against the cliff and Bashir.

Puffs of dirt and chips of stone flew up from the section where the Cardassian lieutenant cowered, too rattled even to return fire. After a moment, Dax realized that the cacophony decomposed into chemical explosions, metallic pings, and the whistle of pellets cutting the air faster than the speed of sound. "Firearms!" she said, howling at the top of her voice for Bashir to hear; "they're shooting *bullets* at 'em!"

What in the world had happened to her peaceful, cow-like Natives? The answer returned in a moment, in a single word: Sisko. "It's Benjamin! Julian, it's Benjamin and the away team—*we're saved!*"

"If the rescue doesn't kill us!" he shouted back, barely audible behind the gunfire.

The battle between the activated Natives and the increasingly demoralized Cardassians lasted forever—that is, eight minutes by Dax's detached, objective count; and the pair of commanders had a ringside seat for the whole show. The Natives sprayed the Cardassians with more gunfire, and at last the soldiers shot back with disruptors . . . that is, until the Natives hurled a thin, uncoiling wire across the enemy defenders. It unrolled blackly against the bright sky, looking almost like oil droplets strung together into a lasso; but within the coil where it fell, disruptors shorted out and melted themselves into slag, taking a few Cardassian paws with them.

The Natives began to drop into the ravine, their puffy, black clothes billowing out like mini-parachutes, slowing their fall just enough to enable them to land unstunned on their feet. They quickly organized into small, four-person *Einsatzgruppen* comprising two people with unwieldy blue-black crossbow-like weapons, one with a device that looked like a hand-held satellite dish with a speaking tube near his mouth, and a chap with a big flour sack in his arms. Dax stared in open-mouthed astonishment at the mopping-up procedure: the dish-antenna man ran foward, whistling into the speaking tube; those Cardassians in the cone of his dish clapped hands over their ears and fell on the ground writhing.

Then one of the crossbowmen stepped forward and fired from ten meters. A black glob streaked through the air, expanding into a fisherman's gill-net en route and falling across the soldiers, tripping them to the ground as they tried to escape.

Finally, the fourth man ran right up to the struggling Cardassians, scooped a big handful of flour from the sack, and flung it across them. The struggles grew weaker and more lethargic, until at last the Cardassian legionaires lay still . . . whether dead or stunned, Dax couldn't tell. *I hope like hell it's the latter,* she thought, dreading the image of Natives as bloodthirsty as Cardassians.

In eight minutes, the battle ended. The only Cardassian left standing was the lieutenant, who raised his hands slowly, staring dumbly from one hooded Native face to another. Dax could read his bitter, astounded expression: this invader was desperately trying to understand how a mindless, gutless, decadent slave-race had leaped from helpless pets to ingenious masters of conflict in *five weeks*.

Dax smiled, shaking her head. *Yeah, I'd like to know that, too.* Then her face turned hard again, as she remembered the massacred Native villages and the butchered old men, women, and children

Then it was over, and the Cardassian taken into

custody. Dax struggled to her feet. The pain in her innards, which she had entirely forgotten about in the heat of battle, returned with a vengeance.

She was just helping Bashir to his foot when a rope snaked down the cliff. A familiar, stocky form appeared, sliding down the rope to land directly next to the pair. "Chief," said Dax, nodding calmly, "so what took you so long?"

"Quark!" bellowed Constable Odo, ferreting out the Ferengi from where he was attempting to scoop some latinum-sparkling reptile eggs into several evidence bags he had borrowed without the constable's knowledge. Irked, Quark held back his response until it became obvious that the changeling had grown subtlely, peering down among the Natives until he found his man.

"Yes, what is is now, Odo?"

"The captain wishes to see you. Immediately."

As he pushed his way forward through the mob, the constable spoke loudly to his back: "Oh, and I will add a count of disturbing a planetary ecosystem to your staggering dossier for this trip alone. Have a *nice* day, Quark."

By the time the Ferengi had reached Sisko, he had already located, in his brain, the ambiguous and vague Federation statutes he intended to rely upon in his defense. "May I direct your attention to Section 282-32 of the . . . I mean, may I help you, Captain?" With an obsequious grin, Quark rubbed away the sweat that had just formed on his lobes.

Sisko said nothing for a moment, staring enigmatically, disconcertingly. "Quark," he began at last, "you will speak to the Cardassian prisoner about a method they have devised for scrubbing the cyanogens out of our systems."

Quark looked closely at the captain and was shocked to realize just how terribly the minor poison had debilitated him. *My profits, Ferengi children learn to tolerate much more active poisons than that in small-count school!* It was just one more example of the frailty of hu-mans . . . and evidently Klingons as well, he judged from a quick glance at a sick and coughing Commander Worf.

"Um . . . why me?" Quark really had no objection; it was a pro-forma complaint.

"Because you are the away team's ambassador-at-large. Since the split-heads negotiation, where you argued so strenuously for that honor."

The Ferengi scowled. He didn't recall the thrust of the conversation to be anything like the captain's version . . . *but he is the captain, and that means he can tell Worf to pound me into the priceless soil up to my upper lobes.* "All right, I'll do it. But I don't have to like it." The divine Ferengi right to kvetch having being defended, Quark toddled off to find the broken, demoralized Cardassian.

The man sat comfortlessly on the broken shard of a boulder, leaning forward, his wedge-shaped trapezius muscles hanging limply from his neck. He stared at a patch of ground that didn't look any more interesting to Quark than all the others, subvocalizing an incessant diatribe about something. The only phrase Quark caught was "fission artillery," which almost sent him right back outside the mob to take his chances with Odo.

"My, my," said the Ferengi, "you do seem to be in a bad position here. An unaccustomed position, having to beg a Starfleet hu-man to be allowed to live."

The lieutenant jerked his head up to stare in cold fury at Quark. "I'd sooner hang than beg anyone for my life!"

Ignoring the response—all Quark had cared about was that he got one, not what it consisted of—he continued. "Still, as the Ferengi say—it might end up a Rule of Acquisition if the FCA gets around to debating it—it's better to live on one's feet than die on one's knees."

The Cardassian lowered his brows and stared, a gorilla trying to cypher out a balance sheet. "No, you've got it backwards. It's better to die on one's knees—"

"And if you're going to live on your feet, you'd better think of something quick. Hurry! Something you can use to bargain with the humans. Much better to strike a deal than beg for charity."

"I mean, to die on one's feet—"

Quark nodded sagely, as if the Cardassian were saying something intelligible instead of gibbering. "Yes, yes, I understand your concern: you think, because you were captured alive when all your command chose instead to fight to the death, that you have nothing left to live for and nothing left to bargain with. None of that inconvenient honor, no men, no latinum." In fact, half his command was alive, intact, and in custody, but Quark skipped lightly over the discrepancy. "But a saying of mine—which will surely someday join the enshrined Rules—says: when you have absolutely nothing, keep it in your pocket; you get a better deal for nothing sight-unseen."

"I don't even know what you're talking about!" The Cardassian leaped to his feet, fists balled, attracting the attention of not a few Native soldiers in addition to Commander Worf, recovered from his coughing fit. Seeing how outnumbered he still was, the captive slowly settled back to his seat, hands raised to prove he was still unarmed.

"But you do have something," said Quark, leaning forward in conspiracy like a lawyer with a mobster client. "And I happen to know the hu-mans will pay a pretty price for it . . . maybe even your life. They want to know how to synthesize that cyanogen-blocker you told Dax about."

The lieutenant froze in mid-rant. His eyes narrowed, and he smiled cruelly. "Oh, at last I understand! I finally detect the point of this pointless discussion. Well, my squat little Ferengi friend, I would rather die myself watching the rest of you croak away your last hours than tell you how to save your miserable lives."

Well, this complicates things, thought Quark. *But what kind of a profitless Ferengi would I be if I let a little setback bankrupt a deal?* "I quite understand. I've made a study of Cardassians, you know. Operating a bar on . . . on *Terok Nor* gives a man plenty of opportunity to observe his neighbors. You're a proud soldier, and you wish you'd been killed in battle rather than captured by these disorderly, ragamuffin Natives."

The lieutenant groaned and stared at Quark's

weskit. Encouraged, the newly minted ambassador continued. "But a deal is like a—a big sword: it cuts in both directions. You think hu-mans don't have secrets, things they don't want anyone to know? You have them bent over the beetle-snuff vat . . . they *have* to pay your price, whatever it is."

The Cardassian prisoner looked much too old to be a mere lieutenant as his pendant indicated. *A long-term noncom who was kicked upstairs beyond his ability?* The man glanced up, trying to parse what Quark had just said. "Any price?"

"My friend, we've got them right where we want them. You struck latinum with that brainstorm, realizing that you could demand any price, any secret at all, in exchange for this one!" Quark couldn't help rubbing his hands with glee. Of course! He should have realized straight away that Cardassians, being a naturally secretive people, are fascinated, even obsessed, with *other people's secrets.* The poor lieutenant, a natural sergeant booted beyond his ability, couldn't possibly resist the deal now. All Quark had to do was close, which meant finding some secret that the soldier desperately wanted to know before he died.

"So let's not skimp on the price we get for our little secret. After all . . ." Quark looked back over his shoulder, then leaned close for the lieutenant's ears alone. "After all, *our* little piece of intelligence literally means *life and death* to the hu-mans. Now, if you could ask just one question, if you could summon up a—a question-answering spirit thing and ask it just one question only, one last thing you want to know, what would it be?"

The old lieutenant closed his eyes and sighed. "The last thing I need to know is . . ." He took a deep breath, moving his lips silently. Then he opened his eyes to stare directly at Quark, cold as Brunt auditing a set of books. "I want to know what happened to Gul Ragat, the—the Gul in command of this whole expedition. Find that out, little man, and I will pay your price, giving you the means to prolong your worthless lives." The Cardassian grinned wickedly. "The technique will bring much joy to your Federation friends, if I know anything about them."

"Uh . . ." Quark licked his lips. "I'll be right back. Don't go anywhere."

Scuttling hurriedly off, the Ferengi started for Captain Sisko, then thought better of it. Quark was absolutely sure they had not encountered the Gul, so the trip would be worthless. There was a slim possibility that Dax and Bashir had information about Gul Ragat. While he tried to find one of them on the off-chance that he actually knew, Quark began devising an elaborate tale of the Gul's heroic last stand, just in case.

Bashir was too busy to talk, trying to synthesize a slightly more potent version of his snake-oil hypospray. When Quark smelled the odor of the doctor's open jars and dishes—the best he could do without a full-scale medical lab—the Ferengi's stomach did a slow roll and he almost lost his lunch. *Small loss,* he conceded; none of them had eaten anything but Cardassian emergency rations—"dire rations," as Quark called them—for nine days. He backed away, trying to reassure himself that it was just the stench of Bashir's concoction, and not the cyanogens affecting his own titanium stomach lining.

He knew instantly where to find Dax. As usual, she was deep in conference with the captain, Worf standing protectively by her side.

"—By radio waves," she was saying. "They've replicated an antenna that can receive them, and they're standing by for your orders."

"Radio waves?" demanded an incredulous Captain Sisko.

"All right, I'm sure Chief O'Brien can jerry-rig something in a few minutes. Worf, start the ball rolling."

"Aye, aye, sir," said the Klingon, stalking away with all the dignity of an operatic hero.

Sisko finally noticed Quark's insistent hand-waving and held up a single finger, meaning hurry up and wait. "Jadzia," said the captain, "was it your idea to plunge into the ocean and play dead?"

She nodded slowly, frowning.

"That," said Sisko, "was a plan worthy of the Emperor Kahless himself—the real one, I mean. I'm going to put you in for a commendation." Then he grinned. "Commendation, hell. I'm going to put you in for a medal!"

Dax tried to hide her emotions, but the Ferengi could tell she was so proud, she *almost* burst her top. *Too bad,* thought Quark with regret.

"Now, Quark," said Sisko, "what did you want to tell me?"

"Nothing. I have to ask Commander Dax something." She barely even noticed Quark, still fixated as she was on a success that wiped out her supposed "failure" at the beginning of the mission. Quark had never felt quite so small and insignificant as he did just then, but he got over it quickly and back to his old self. "Jadzia," he said, appealing to the friend, not the commander, "the prisoner wants to know what happened to Gul—Gul—"

"Ragat?" she asked.

"Yes, that's it. How did you know?" Quark winked. "I think we can get the formula out of him for curing this cyanogen damage. Wouldn't *that* be a kick in the seat to Dr. Bashir?"

Dax drew back a step. "He . . . wants to know what happened to Gul Ragat?"

It's always a bad sign when you ask a question and they repeat it back to you, thought Quark nervously. "You actually know this Gul?"

"Well, in a manner of speaking."

"What do you mean, in a manner of speaking?"

"I mean Yes, I guess. I do know him, and I know what we did—what happened to him."

"Uh-oh. Tell me he's not dead."

"He's not dead."

Quark sighed. "All right, then tell me what happened to him."

She was hiding something. Quark noted the distance she had gotten between them, the way she rubbed her forefinger against her thumb, licked her lips, glanced away from Quark, as if lost in thought, but really unable to meet his gaze. "I, uh, don't think your lieutenant is going to be dancing for joy when you tell him what . . . what we did. What I did. What Julian and I did, but it's my responsibility."

"Well, Old Man?" demanded the captain. "Are

you going to tell us, or should we wait for the holoplay?" He was being humorous, but Quark had a suspicion there was also some real consternation.

"We marooned him, Benjamin."

"Marooned him where?"

"In the desert. With some water and food. He can walk his way out—if he lives."

Quark's jaw fell open. "Mar . . . mar-*ooned?* You left him all alone in the middle of a bunch of sand dunes, a thousand kilometers from the nearest water? And I'm supposed to trade *this* for a formula to save your miserable hides?" Angrily, shook both fists as her. *"Commander,* you just don't know how lucky you are that I'm a Ferengi businessman, because any other kind of ambassador would have thrown himself on a Native petard about now!"

He crunched back toward the prisoner, feeling the fortune in latinum squish past his boots. *Why can't everyone else be as simple and easy to bribe as a Ferengi,* he thought, *instead of an incomprehensible joint account of insanity, honor, spite, and greedlessness?*

CHAPTER
14

Water was seeping up from somewhere. It conspired to send Quark sprawling, but he kept on his feet only by an economic miracle. It infiltrated his boots and infested his pants legs. The perfect metaphor for the mess he found himself mired in: persuading a sharp Cardassian lieutenant to swap the life-giving biochemical information he had for the horrible, horrible story Quark possessed.

When the Ferengi saw the prisoner, still stuck to his rocky stump as if glued, Quark had the inspiration to forget all about the marooned Gul and tell instead his own brilliant concoction, the heroic last stand of Gul Ragat the Bold but Very Unlucky. But some nagging voice stopped him. *Am I growing a conscience? Profits, what a handicap for a successful businessman!* But fortune smiled, and Quark, upon deep reflection, decided it was the voice of skepticism, instead.

What if the lieutenant, who was not exactly stupid, figured out that Quark was lying? There were so many details to get wrong, so many ways the mark—the customer—could realize he was being lied to by the vendor. There simply were too many uncertainties in the transaction for proper product placement. Visions of what an enraged Cardassian could do before being brought down by phaser fire made him swallow hard.

Quark, feeling trapped and quite the fool, was forced to tell the truth—because anything else, no matter how plausible, was as likely to expose him as cover his backside. heavy-lobed The Ferengi opened fire on the Cardassian with all his ammunition of argument and dickering, setting the deal in concrete before revealing even one speck of actual information: the lieutenant was *not* going to be able to slither out of his end of the deal.

Quark knew going in what he would gain and lose; if humans were unpredictable, Cardassians were all *too* predictable. In the end, by a tortuous path of negotiation, bargaining chips, covert hints, and overt threats, they ended at a straight-up swap, story for story . . . exactly as Quark had expected.

And one final indignity: "But you go first," said the Cardassian, curling his lip and snorting like Odo . . . *is that where the constable got it from, all those Cardassians who raised him?* "I would never trust an honorless Ferengi to keep his side of a bargain."

Quark sighed. He had anticipated that, too. But he put on a show of beaten resignation.

"Honorless! Was ever a people more put-upon than we?" Quark shook his head at the heavens, where the Cardassian ships had recently engaged in some terrible battle, if Chief O'Brien were right. "Odo, Sisko, Brunt, and now you! Does *everyone in the quadrant* have to impugn my integrity? Has it become the intragalactic sport? Fine. You may not trust me, but I, the most trusting man in the Alpha Quadrant, will even trust you, a Cardassian prisoner of war." Shaking his head at the folly of the universe, Quark told the sordid tale—the truthful one—the sad, wretched tale of the Gul who was sent packing.

When he had finished, he took a step back, preparing to duck, dodge, and run like hell as the lieutenant digested the fate of his commander and reacted according to his conscience. At first the prisoner looked down at the ground. Then he caught himself and his low-class posture and straightened up, his expression still unreadable. But by the time he turned to face Quark, the "neutral, haughty stare," as the Ferengi termed the default Cardassian face, was beginning to crack, the bright shimmer of a faint smile peeking through.

Cold creeps coiled in Quark's stomach. It was insane, but . . . the Cardassian lieutenant was actually grinning like a loon at the ignominious end of his commander.

The still-anonymous prisoner burst into loud guffaws. Desperately, he tried to stifle the unseemly display, but it was out of control. Before Quark could extract any information about the process, the prisoner was doubled over in hysterical but muzzled laughter. "Oh, I wish, I wish, I could have seen his face when you marooned him by the lake!"

Putting on his bartender's cap, Quark joined in the joke, slapping the prisoner on the back and laughing his altruistic head off until the man calmed down. Then he started asking questions, sliding them in between laughs as loud and inarticulate as the yelps of the female split-heads when "Arrk fly."

The Cardassian was generous, more than Quark would have expected from that normally tight-lipped species. In fifteen minutes, Quark extracted the formula for protecting them, once and for all, against the deadly atmospheric contaminants. His only worry, as he licked sharp, pointed teeth and rubbed his hands together, was that the technique would so horrify Captain Sisko and the rest that they might just possibly not be able to bring themselves to implement it—though it made the Ferengi's mouth water and his wallet long for Ferenginar, visions of fresh Huyperian beetle-snuff dancing between his lobes.

Chief O'Brien tried desperately not to think of the dilemma that faced them. He found as many bits and pieces of Dax's tricorder as he could—it had been blown to bits, along with the Cardassian skimmers, more the pity, when she left it behind as the Native shelling started. He helped Odo, Worf, and a detachment of Natives bury the Cardassian bodies . . . that, at least, O'Brien could do with a clear conscience and a song in his heart, after the horrors he had seen them commit: the invasion, the massacres, even the murder of children hardly older than Molly. *Sure, I'll be having no nightmares tonight,* he promised grimly. The sheep had turned tables, and nobody would weep for the wolves.

But he had begun coughing up blood. His intestines burned with terrible gas pains that brought him to his knees twice during the burial. Even the cones in his retinas had ceased to function, as Bashir explained, restricting the chief's vision to an eerie world of dim black and white. It was harder to think, to concentrate; thoughts slithered around inside his skull like leaves swirling in a windstorm, and he grabbed for them with both hands: *I'm dying,* was one such thought. . . . Another—*they can save us* . . . but a third came—*we can't take one to save another.*

He grunted as a Native tried to push him out of the grave he was digging in the swampy, latinum-thick soil. A group of them had taken a few minutes to invent a back-hoe, and they wanted him to step aside so they could dig the holes more efficiently. Through the midday gloom of his own eyeballs, O'Brien saw the Natives were already rolling the Drek'la corpses into the graves two or three at a time, with no more ceremony than one would give a fish buried for fertilizer. The prisoners sill alive showed no more concern for their own dead than did the Natives.

He didn't object to the anonymous burials . . . these butchers deserved it. But he desperately needed the physical labor, to think through the moral morass: *Should we grind up the blessed lizards and eat them?*

To a moral man like Miles Edward O'Brien, father and warrior, builder and destroyer, the idea that he could save his own life only by killing an innocent sentient being was abhorrent. But he *was* a father, and a husband, and a builder, and a warrior. People needed him. They relied upon him. *Without me,* he thought, blushing at such seeming egotism even within his own mind, *there's a lot of folk will die in this war that wouldn't be likely to if I'm there.* His engineer's mind compelled him to speak the truth—even to himself.

The news brought by the grinning Quark had stunned the entire away team. The only way discovered by the Cardassians to protect against further deterioration of their pulmonary and nervous systems—the dying of the cones in O'Brien's eyes was only the most "visible" sign of a deteriorating brain—was to grind up the Praying Lizards, as the chief dubbed them, and extract a long-chain biopolymer that scrubbed the system of cyanogens, at least in the concentrations produced by breathing. ('It won't save your life if you eat the native food," added the Cardassian lieutenant cheerfully.)

The problem, of course, was that the lizards, like every other form of semi-advanced life on Sierra-Bravo, were *sentient.* According to Dax and Bashir, who had seen information ripped from a Cardassian tap into the planet's core computer system, intelligence and consciousness had been genetically engineered into the species for some horrific, Frankensteinian experiment. *The whole damned planet is an experiment* . . . another fluttering-leaf thought that the chief managed to catch and hold long enough to understand it.

Actually, the biopolymer could be extracted from any "animal" more advanced than those lizards . . . but they would be even more sentient—closer to full humanity than the Prayers. And all the less advanced creatures were just as susceptible to the cyanogens as were humans, Cardassians, and other invaders: they simply lived such a short time that most died of other causes long before the contaminants could kill them. Nonlaboratory rats rarely died of cancer either—because they didn't live long enough to contract it.

Chief O'Brien looked around and discovered Captain Sisko in conference with Dax, Odo, and Worf. The chief blinked; he had no idea when the last two had left their grave-digging jobs. But straining his failing brain, he vaguely remembered the captain asking him to join the conference some time ago . . . a minute? A day? *I said something about coming as soon as—as I finished—digging something. Something? A grave, as soon as I finished digging another Cardassian grave.*

Sighing, O'Brien stood and stretched his aching, stooped shoulders. He laid the folding shovel next to the hole and allowed Owena-da and the overly muscular Rimtha-da to pluck him from the hole. The back-hoe roared behind the chief, tearing a scream from his throat before he remembered that he *had* seen it before . . . just a few minutes ago, in fact.

Oh, God . . . I am in bad shape. My mind is almost gone! Fear pricked at his spine, and made him pick up his feet and hustle to the conference.

Quark was missing; he was rounding up as many Prayers as he could . . . in case they decided to use the Cardassian formula. Dax and Bashir were desperately trying to synthesize the biopolymer, using samples from the cackling, giggling prisoner. It was a hopeless task without a complete ship's medical lab, the nearest one being at the moment submerged on the *Defiant,* days of travel distant even by Native trucks. Bashir's best judgment was that they would not survive—not even Worf, who was finally himself sucumbing to the cyanogen's cellular destructiveness. Only Quark, the prisoner, and of course Odo (who had no biology) would likely make it back to the ship. For some reason, the Ferengi anatomy was much less susceptible to poison or contaminants. *Probably from thousands of years of practice,* thought O'Brien.

Too bad about the skimmers, he thought; *they might've spared us the moral dilemma.*

When he staggered into the circle, Worf immediately grabbed him by the arm and injected him with some hypospray. After a few moments, O'Brien's head cleared somewhat—at the expense of his pulse and heartbeat racing, blood pressure soaring, and waves of anxiety and panic coursing through his veins: Worf had shot him full of epinephrine, causing a burst of adrenaline to flood his circulatory system.

"People," said an equally shaky Captain Sisko, sounding not much like his old, confident self, "we have only a short time left to decide. Julian . . . Julian tells me that if the brain damage is extending—extensive enough, it *won't matter* whether we get the bio—biopolymer. We'll be diminished per-ma-nent-ly."

The captain closed his eyes, and a tear rolled down his cheek. The thought that even Benjamin Sisko was deteriorating mentally and emotionally sent a fresh and stronger wave of terror through Chief O'Brien. *God, if he goes, we're all bloody doomed!* He knew that his own emotions were under siege. But far from reassuring him, that only made the panic worse. He fought it down, pushing harder with his own will than he ever had before.

Sisko appeared to bear down on himself, regaining some control from his damaged neurons. "We must decide *now*, men. I have Bashir's and the Old Man's opinions, and I'm keeping them in my pocket until I hear what the rest of you say."

O'Brien couldn't shake the absurd image of Jadzia Dax in one of the captain's pockets and the doctor in the other. It distracted him . . . but it was better than the artificial feeling of panic. "Sir," he said, speaking too quickly because of the epinepherine, "how do we know when we decide that we're not just letting dead brains and bodies full of adrenaline make the choice?"

Worf snarled instead of speaking. The epinephrine brought out violence instead of fear in the warrior. "I will make no decision based on some chemical in my blood!"

"Silence, Worf," said Sisko. Even in his condition, the command tone caught the Klingon's attention.

"The chief raises a valid concern. But the time for guilt and worry is after we decide—not before."

"Captain," said Constable Odo, "the first rule for any animal species is survival."

"But we're not animals!" said O'Brien, feeling a surge of irrational fury at the changeling. "Or we're beyond animals, whatever you call it. This is an intelligent species we're talking about killing and eating."

"Technically," said Odo, retreating into lecture mode, "we would not be eating the Praying Lizards. Bashir would terminate them, pulverize their bodies, and extract the biopolymer for injection via hypospray."

The chief wrapped his arms around a head that suddenly burned, as if a red-hot bowl had just been slapped over his skull. "I don't know as I can eat an intelligent life-form to save myself!" He realized he was screaming, and struggled to calm down.

"Perhaps," said Odo, oddly sympathetic, "considering the moral implications, each person should choose for himself whether he is willing."

"No," said Sisko, eyes closed. O'Brien held his breath. "I will make the decision for all. It is my responsibility."

The captain doesn't want there to be any confusion at the inquest—and there will be one. He's going to take the medicine for us, every swallow.

Dax squatted, wrapping her arms around herself. After the chief himself, she was the most affected, either because she had swallowed Sierra-Bravo seawater, or maybe because she was a female. *Or maybe Trills are just more susceptible,* thought O'Brien, his perforated mind wandering. *Wonder why Ferengi are so little affected?*

Captain Sisko took a long look around at each of his team: Commander Worf, struggling to shrug off the effects, ignoring the pain, but unable to stop the shimmy in his hands, the trembling in his knees; Commander Dax, hurting, unable to stand, equally unable to complain or give in; "Ambassador" Quark, doubtless glad to be a Ferengi but looking worried, as if nervous about what bloody thoughts the rest of the team had for him—and about whether he, too, would soon begin to suffer the physical and mental deterioration of the cyanogens; his nemesis, Constable Odo, shuffling uncomfortably, surely fretting at seeing so many friends on the point of death or permanent brain damage, but already thinking, O'Brien was certain, of what he would have to do to rescue some or all of them if they collapsed on the way back to the *Defiant;* poor, apologetic Dr. Julian Bashir, the superior man rendered helpless, angry, distraught by a tiny molecule that eluded even his genetically enhanced brain, eye, and hand.

"And poor, sick me," added Chief Miles Edward O'Brien, vocalizing half-aloud. *The fighting man, the warrior, the strong man who is brought lower than any of the others, even Dax.* Whatever shreds of masculine pride the poison had left O'Brien were blown away like pollen by his oversensitive reaction to it.

"Quark," said Sisko, his voice the croak of a frog, "I've decided. We're going to—"

"Hold on, Captain." Dr. Bashir put in. He was

holding Chief O'Brien's tricorder. "I've run an analysis on the polymer that makes up the cyanogen scrubber. The Cardassians would have had no way of knowing this—and I'm a little surprised to find it out myself—but it's the same polymer some of the plants are made out of, at least in part."

"You mean," Sisko said, "that all this time we've had the answer and didn't know it?"

"Yes," the Doctor said. "That's what I'm saying. Funny how things work out sometimes, isn't it?"

Quark said, "Just curious, but what decision had you made? Was it us or the lizards?"

"It must be the mental impairment," Sisko said, smiling, "but I'm afraid I can't recall."

CHAPTER
15

THIRTY YEARS AGO

CRESTING THE long, high, steep, slippery bridge across the Swifts, Sister Winn paused. Grand spires laughed in the shimmer, binding a red-peaked roof, except where missing tiles had been replaced by gray Cardassian preforms. Walls bulged outward, sagging beneath the weight of four centuries, next to a lawn half-dead but stubbornly maintained, the same losing battle fought when Rald Mirana ruled the roost as president of the General Lyll Military Academy, before Winn's grandmother was born. The Cardassians, out of respect for a soldier, had not renamed the school.

The iron sky brought out the dark, precious-green trees—blue or azure would have drowned the muted color. *How somber a tone,* thought the sister, *for a step-off into the arms of the Prophets.*

"My chest," she gasped, clutching herself. The

201

vision of the pain was so vivid, she almost felt it. "Let me sit, my gracious lord." Not waiting for a response, she plumped down on the railing of the bridge.

Gul Ragat said nothing, but he stopped and looked away from her. She watched him without being observed herself. Ragat was a youngster, barely into his twenties, trying hard to be a man older than his time. Grayness set about his skin like powder makeup, dusting his cheeks with pallor, his eyes with dimness, so they had no sparkle of life. *He knows, he senses that his career is at an end,* she thought—and she felt nothing, not a twinge of conscience.

Gul Ragat was not a man well-liked by his fellow Cardassian generals. Migar tolerated him because the legate had grown up with "the old Gul," Ragat's father Ragat First. But Migar was an eggshell blown clean of its contents. Soon he would crumble in upon himself, and Gul Dukat, master of *Terok Nor,* the station of death that had proven itself so effective in the few years it had been in orbit, would step into Migar's place.

Dukat despised Ragat. He despised Ragat's family, his easy grace, his youth, his class. Everyone had heard the rumors about Dukat and Bajoran women—even the Bajorans. There was even talk of a child somewhere, a mix, a half-breed . . . but Sister Winn found the thought so profoundly disturbing that she refused to credit it. Powerful though Dukat was—and he controlled the Cardassian army of occupation the way Migar never had—he would never be accepted in a society that accepted Ragat.

Ragat was Old School; Dukat was the New Cardassian. *And I have just handed Dukat my lord's head in a golden chalice,* thought the priestess with a grim smile and not a shred of guilt. Having been caught at the open door of the code room, Winn would be executed—even if Dukat, by some bizarre twist of destiny, actually *believed* her lie that she had never looked inside. And as she had been Gul Ragat's closest Bajoran servant, her blood would leave an indelible stain on Ragat's career. Nothing so crass as a court-martial, just the low whisper in a stretched ear, the frown, the glance away, the too-stiff, too-formal politeness in Ragat's presence, and the smirk behind the back of a hand . . . enough so that Ragat would be finished—and he knew it.

He knows there's nothing he can do about it. I wonder how bitter he feels? Enough, she thought, seeing the first ray of light, *that he might give way to compassion?*

She sat on the wall of the crescent, now called the Colonel Gorak Mahak Bridge. Beneath her, the waters of the aptly named Swifts rushed and swirled, flying over rocks and rolling boulders by night. Chubby priestesses were not generally known for being excellent swimmers . . . but most hadn't grown up hard against the Shakiristi River, as Sister Winn had.

A young Gul could be excused for making the mistake of underestimating her. So many others had.

The thoughts may have come direct from the Prophets; certainly Sister Winn would forever say they had, assuming forever were longer than the time it took to drown. But the guts, she knew, were her own, a remnant from her wilder days as a child at the convent school, when she got into so much mischief that the Mother Superior, Sister Opaka before she made vedek, threatened to endow a special punishment chair in Winn's name.

Clutching her chest and gasping in what must have seemed like astonished agony, Winn opened her eyes as wide as saucers and allowed her face to turn distinctly white. Gul Ragat turned—how could he not?—and asked, in some alarm, "Winn, Winn, what's wrong?"

Slowly, Winn allowed her head to fall backward. She had never seen a person die from a heart attack, but she had an excellent imagination. She put it to good use.

Before any of her guards could react, Sister Winn toppled backwards off the Colonel Gorak Mahak and into the Swifts. The river was cold, and for an instant, she thought the shock really would kill her! The rush dragged her under, catching her robes of office with ice-hands, wrapping snow-arms around her ample circumferance, pulling her to the bottom of the flow with chains so cold they burned her flesh.

She had caught a good breath, and she knew how long she could hold it—on solid ground at room temperature. Tumbling along the frigid bottom of the Swifts, she lost her lungfull in moments, but she refused to surface. Instead, damning modesty, she slithered out of the clothing that held her fast.

Winn forced open her eyes; the river was not so deep that it became opaque, and she could see well enough for a few swim-strokes in every direction, despite clouds of sand whipped into a froth by the water's churn. She knew what to look for and soon found it: a stand of broomsticks growing along the bank, marching right into the water.

Seeing stars flashing against the blackness of her vision, she pumped for the reeds. Drums beat and roared in her ears—*my pulse?* It sounded as if it would burst the sides of her head in a moment.

The Swifts cooperated, throwing her into the broomstick stand with a vicious chuckle. She grabbed an armful, halting her tumble and nearly wrenching her arms from their sockets.

Winn's lungs were heaving. It took every molecule of will not to open her mouth and suck in riverwater. With faltering strength, she tried to snap the largest reed off at its base.

Forget it . . . don't be an ass! It's much too thick for you, even for a muscular young man. Never one to argue with reality, Winn, obedient to the voice, chose a much thinner reed and broke that one instead, clamping her hand quickly over the bottom to minimize the water she would have to swallow.

Holding onto a small clump of broomsticks with her twined feet, she twisted face-up and wrestled the reed into place over her mouth, jamming it past her lips. It was a nightmare forcing herself to *swallow* the water inside before taking her first breath. But she had long experience suppressing her natural reactions. She was, after all was said, a spy for the Resistance.

The first gasp of air tasted sweeter than cake. The second, third, tenth calmed her nerves. By the time a minute had elapsed, she was aware enough to wonder whether Gul Ragat's men would swiftly pluck her out of the flow and haul her, streaming water, to the transporters at the Academy. It would be no trick to find her. Even if none of the guards had a scanner, one could run to the Academy and be back in a few minutes.

She waited, counting seconds as accurately as she could, until ten minutes passed. She was so chilled that her bones felt about to crack. Then she counted all over again. By that time, she understood: Ragat had *let her go*. He had allowed her to die in peace, in her own time, on her own planet, not by Gul Dukat's schedule on *Terok Nor*. Ragat gave her that much respect . . . and had happily stolen the equivalent satisfaction from Gul Dukat.

It was the single courageous, decent act she had ever seen her "master" perform . . . she almost regretted what he would suffer in her place. Almost.

She stayed another five minutes, just to be sure. Then, holding her broomstick as high as she could, Sister Winn loosed her leg-grip and let the Swifts carry her along wherever the Prophets pleased, to cast her ashore some way downstream. When she beached up on a sandbar, Winn took it as a sign. She let her air tube float away on the current and stood, instantly regretting that she hadn't saved the reed for a walking stick. But she hardly needed it, for she heard Bajoran voices less than a hundred strides from the river. She followed the curses, never before having been so happy to hear oaths and blasphemies, and discovered three mechanics trying to repair a truck engine that had stalled.

It took Sister Winn five weeks to hook up with the

nearest Resistance cell, which was led by a man who called himself Jaras Shie. Five weeks of skulking through woods dark and deep, skirting all habitation, looking for the secret blazes, "random" rockfalls, and other signs of a nearby cell. She begged some men's clothing from the mechanics to hide her nakedness but had to walk on bare feet the whole time. By the time she found the spot to wait for (and be observed by) the cell scouts, her feet were toughened from rock and twig, and she had lost much of her fleshy excess baggage.

She was blindfolded, searched, and led a tortuous path to the cell meeting, where she met "Jaras," whoever he really was. She began to tell her story— not her perilous escape, but the important information about the holocam and what she had seen in the code room—when a man in the circle surrounding her shouted as if the fire had suddenly burned his feet. He tore off his black hood and ran up to her, an old man who smelled of fish.

Winn froze in amazement and beatific grace. The fisherman was the same she had seen in the temple in Riis, far up the road, into whose pack she had slipped the holocam. She recovered her aplomb quickly. "Indeed," she said, speaking very much like her old self, "the Prophets do move in mystery and humor."

They threw her a feast, and she overdid and got sick. But every moment was precious to her that night, and for long years to come. The intelligence was used with care, and it was half a lifetime before it was all used up. The Cardassians never did discover what they had lost and what Bajor had won.

Gul Ragat was recalled to Cardassia Prime, and Sister Winn never heard of him again. But by then, she was a busy woman, studying for her vedek examinations; and she wasn't really listening anyway.

Ops, Level One, slid into Kira's view evil-quick. She felt like an undead Bajoran ghost popping up out of the grave, clutching the death of Bajor in her one good arm. She limped off the turbolift platform carrying the portable, far-seeing anomaly, also known as the Orb, sealed in its latching cabinet. It felt wrong, but then everything felt wrong lately: Kira's entire life had gone awry, beginning the moment Captain Sisko and the Federation decided to hand over the station for a "trial run" of independence to a people they evidently thought of as too childish to be trusted.

Wasn't there a human ghost who walked "With 'er 'ead tucked underneath 'er arm"? It sounded familiar, but her mind was wandering. Squinting through her swollen eyes, Kira mustered what dignity she could to shuffle forward with the horrible ransom.

Was it really worth a hundred lives? A thousand? It was hard for the major to believe it. To Kira, the Orbs *were* Bajor, and Bajor's population was numbered in the billions! But Kira herself had no stomach for the death-decision, either. She had proven that when she yielded to the blackmail of Jake, Keiko, Molly, and Kirayoshi—who were mercifully absent, having served their purpose. She was sure they were but a few levels away, ready to be hauled back if Kira or Winn were suddenly to grow a spine.

"Here'sh your portable, far-sheeing . . . your damned Orb." Kira stretched her arm, offering the cabinet to the dean without even a glance at Kai Winn. But the Kai swept her hand out in a lightning thrust that made Kira blink. The old woman intercepted the handoff, holding the box to her bosom, a new mother nursing her child.

"I will give it to the dean, Major," said Winn, softly but firmly. "It is my right as Kai, not yours, child." It was an ugly performance, and Kira felt dirtied by the Kai's obsequious eagerness to please.

Kira let her hands fall limp. She was close to vomiting, but she swallowed it back down. She couldn't afford to be distracted by anything, certainly not nausea.

"Show me," whispered the dean. His voice was hoarse with excitement . . . the first emotion Kira could recall hearing from him during the entire occupation. He literally trembled with anxious impatience, clutching greedily for the box.

Kai Winn deftly evaded the dean's grasping hands. "I will show it to you, my friend. But it's too complex to go into now. Let's adjourn to my office." Winn nodded up toward what Kira would always think of as the captain's ready-room.

"Let me see it *now!*" At the last word, the dean's voice rose to a piercing wail, sending Kira reeling back a step in astonishment and disgust.

Winn sighed. "As you wish." She carefully unlatched the doors of the box, opening them wide and flashing the dean with the innards. Kira stared like a starving beggar at a banquet, seeing the Orb, she imagined for the last time.

Once they get their claws on it, she reckoned, *they'll trade it to the Dominion for an end to their duties as prison guards—unconvicted "prisoners"— and that would give them access to the Prophets, for whatever deadly plan they had in mind.*

"You will come with us into the office," said the faceless dean, still admiring the Orb-box and its contents. "You will activate the portable, far-seeing anomaly yourself and demonstrate its use to contact the wormhole aliens."

"It is not difficult," said the Kai. "You merely probe the Orb with a high-frequency burst of six GigaHertz electromagnetic radiation."

Radiation? Burst? Kira was confused. She had never thought of the Orb as a microwave receiver before. *What the bloody hell is she talking about?*

And then Kai Winn closed the box, but she turned it around to do so, giving Major Kira her first glimpse inside. Her eyes widened, her mouth dropped; she sucked in a sharp gasp, which she passed off by instantly making the sign of the Prophets on her forehead and looking down in consternation . . . for the bright, shiny, silver sphere she had seen in the box in no way resembled the real Orb, not in the least.

Kai Winn had slipped them a ringer.

The shock almost sent Kira to the floor with dizziness. Her face whitened as she desperately tried to digest the new information: *Everything I thought was wrong! Every damned, blessed thing . . . I've had it all backwards, she's not—the Kai didn't—* But if the cabinet didn't contain an Orb, as clearly it did not, then what the *hell* was in that box?

"You will activate the anomaly," insisted the dean. "If you make an attempt to damage it, you will be instantly killed. Then the second-ranking prisoner will operate the anomaly in your place. You will follow."

"I will follow," agreed Winn instantly. One by one, the Liberated climbed to the upper part of the Ops level, heading toward the ready-room. Kai Winn lowered her face and began to pray silently, her lips moving as she intoned the well-known prayer for the ending.

Kira heard an insistent ringing in her ears: something the Kai had said about a *special project,* something involving the Orb, looking for the Orb, something. At once, the twisted, tangled pattern sharpened into the spider-web lines of a crystal goblet: the "special project" was *not* to find the Orb . . . with a gasp, Kira realized that Kai Winn had somehow managed to instruct her elite guard to *construct a counterfeit Orb.*

Kira looked up, staring at the Kai with an intensity of emotion she had never before felt toward the woman. If the silver sphere were not an Orb, not a real one, then it could only, Kira reasoned, be one other thing. Anything else would be discovered quickly, and they would be right back to the porridge course of the feast of suffering of the Bajoran and Federation inhabitants.

The silver sphere was a bomb. And Kai Winn was about to follow them up to the ready room and commit suicide to drain the deception to its bitter dregs.

At last, Kira's mind jerked back onto the course it

should have followed from the beginning of the occupation, and her feet finally became unstuck from the floor. At her feet lay still the broken handle of the ratageena mug with its jagged, sharp shard for stabbing . . . stabbing not to execute, not in response to betrayal, but to save a life, one among many. Kira swiftly stooped, ignoring the pain and the blurry vision, and caught the handle in her one good hand.

"Die, you traitor!" Kira lunged forward, again catching by surprise the complacent aliens, who were used to dealing with demoralized convicted criminals who complied with their own captivity.

The blade-like piece slid easily into the Kai's shoulder. She yelped in surprise, and then the pain struck, hurling her to the ground in agony. Kira felt not the slightest taste of remorse despite a hand coated with a thick sauce of blood. She bent low over the Kai's ear as the guards turned with their ultra-fast reaction time and bolted back down the ladder-way. "Kai, Kai," she said urgently in Winn's ear, "hang on: as a wise woman once said, what we can tolerate, we can endure.

"Endure, my Kai. It will be over soon, I promise."

Winn looked back at Kira with an odd light of intelligence. Then the blood-loss, the shock, and the pain conspired to put the Kai's lights out. An instant later, Kira was buried beneath a swarm of prison guards. Her last thought before the event was, *I wonder whether a double-thick layer of the Liberated will shield me from the blast?*

CHAPTER
16

Kira could see virtually nothing under the dogpile. She could barely breathe. She already had at least one broken rib from the beating, and an agonizing ripping feeling in her chest indicated that the broken ends had lacerated her flesh. *I wonder if they punctured a lung?* she thought dully, and wondered also why she no longer seemed to care much.

Through a gap between the legs of one of the Liberated piled on top of her, Kira just caught a glimpse of a guard standing over Kai Winn. They both dematerialized—*in the infirmary, please the Prophets!*

Kira tried to resist being crushed, but she had no strength left, she had lost it all, to depression, to enforced servility, apathy, and now physical abuse. Slowly, she settled, spreading across the deck, heedless of both the searing pain in her chest and her inability to suck in enough air. *Will I pass out before being blown to bits?*

She heard the clanking of boots on the Cardassian metal ladderway, as the dean and his top lieutenants reclimbed back to the ready-room. If he issued orders about Kira or the Kai, he did so silently, as was his wont, for Kira heard nothing. But the guards piled atop her did not make a move, either to lift her up or execute her. She could only guess what the dean was planning . . . not that he would get much of a chance to execute his plan if the Kai were as competent at direct action as she was at political action.

Major Kira of the Bajoran Defense Forces and the Federation, executive officer of *Emissary's Sanctuary* and *Deep Space Nine,* resistance fighter against Cardassian and Liberated, closed her eyes and offered what she assumed was her final prayer to the Prophets. Curiously, she felt no rush of religious certainty or ecstasy; her prayers were as detached and formalistic as they often were when she was stressed, angry, or doubt-ridden. She tried to review her life, but she couldn't think of any great accomplishments: all she could think was that she never had loved a man the way she had hoped to love, never been the hero she'd imagined in her girlhood, never served Bajor the intense way a Bajoran so desperately desired. *If I loved at all, I loved Bajor. All else was mere physical desire, comfort, and custom.* The thought repelled, when it should have exalted.

She heard a muffled pop. *It's the fuse. The explosion will come any instant!*

What, she pondered, would she have done if she

had another few years to do it? *I would have gotten away from the damned station for a while. Mabye toured restored Bajor, rest on my laurels a bit. Oddly, even in this extreme circumstance, the idea was unappealing.*

Kira caught herself making a list of all the people she wished she could talk to before dying. A few she wanted to say goodbye to, to one or two she wished she could apologize. By far, the Prophets' share were people she wanted to punch in the nose or kick in the groin. *How elevated!* But, she sighed, that was the complex bundle of neuroses that was Kira Nerys.

In fact, the guards on her back were *awfully* still. Preternaturally so. Curious, Kira shifted herself, shifted her legs, just to see what would happen, but nothing did; there was no response whatsoever.

She jerked, pulling one arm free. She pushed at one of the bodies above her, but it didn't react, didn't respond, made no attempt to recapture her arm. And at once, the certainty flooded Kira that *everybody was dead.* She lay beneath a heaping pile of dead bodies.

Filled with a surge of panic and horror, Kira's body went into a convulsion, ignoring the fire in her chest. She screamed—twice. Long before she dug her way out, the panic subsided, but her determination intensified. Two or three minutes passed before she finally made free.

She squirmed free and pulled herself erect, clinging to the comm panel as to a life preserver, and stared in stunned incomprehension at the tangle of corpses. "What the—?" The rest of her epithet would have turned her mother's ears bright red. Kira stared around Ops in complete confusion. Dead Liberated bodies lay everywhere in positions indicating they had died in an instant where they stood, collapsing to the floor in positions that indicated broken bones and even a split skull in one case, where the guard had fallen against the sharp, angry, Cardassian corner of O'Brien's engineering well. *Maybe we should put ProtectiFoam on those edges,* she thought, not even noticing the inanity.

"Or *are you* dead?" She left the security of the communications panel and stumbled to a body that was not part of the mob atop her. She stooped, catching the floorplates to prevent falling as her dizziness overwhelmed her. She examined the body one-handedly. "Just as I thought . . . it's an alien. And I have no idea how to tell whether it's alive or dead."

She shook off the vertigo and lethargy and moved as quickly as she could for the ladderway. She had to grit her teeth against the tearing in her chest, but at least she was breathing better. Kira decided she hadn't punctured a lung; it had just been the weight crushing her down.

She felt a curious reluctance to enter the readyroom, as if she might not be worthy to enter Captain Sisko's most personal sanctorum. "Oh, come on, Kira, you've been in here a thousand times." But it was the first time since the occupation, and she was not entirely confident of her performance under that duress. But there would be time to examine herself and her actions . . . now she needed to know *what had happened.* Kira opened the door to a scene out of hell.

No fewer than nine dead Liberated bodies surrounded the center of the room. The bodies were pushed against the wall and injured, as by a blast. But clearly, to Kira's practiced eye, they were not slain by the force: the damage was too light. They were all, however, as dead as dead could be, and their faces—they were definitely not helmets, she realized that at last—were gray. She touched one face and it crumbled inward like ash.

Then she recovered her aplomb and examined the rest of the bodies—without touching. They all showed evidence of some sort of burning, but a burning without flames or scorching. Then she looked at the "Orb" in the center, on the captain's desk, and she understood. The "special project" item that the Kai's team had constructed—not found—was a bomb . . . but a very special kind. Kira had studied her own military history as well as that of Cardassia, the Federation, even the Klingon Empire. All had at one time or another come up with the clever idea of a bomb that killed people but left buildings and documents intact.

Winn had ordered the construction of a *neutron bomb* with a microwave trigger. The dean had just solved his own problem of what to do with his life, as well as the problems of the rest of the occupied station.

The station! Kira spun, darted out of the ready room, and slid down the ladderway like an ensign in a sailing-ship holoplay, falling at the end when she forgot and tried to grab with her left hand. *But why didn't I die, along with everyone else?* The Kai had doubtless set the range of the neutron bomb to a small radius, a few meters. Surely she wouldn't kill the entire station! And that meant that the rest of the Liberated, scattered throughout *Deep Space Nine*, were still alive and armed, and probably wondering why their communicators had suddenly grown silent. Soon, after being unable to raise the dean, they would venture up to Ops to see for themselves what had happened. Kira had only a tiny window of vulnerability before they recaptured Ops and regained control.

Because I was *at the bottom of a pile of armored and shielded bodies.* Their radiation shielding was insufficient, in one layer, to protect them from death. But several layers of it, as well as layers of bodies, were enough to protect Kira herself . . . though she doubtless must have some radiation damage Bashir or somebody would have to fix. At the moment, however, she was alive and mobile.

She scrambled to the Security console; within ten seconds she had completely cut off the shields. She could have done it in an instant if the Liberated hadn't made their own minor improvements to the system. But with the shields down, there was nothing to stop the *Harriman*, nothing to stop Captain Taggart from beaming aboard a huge strike force. The leaderless, frightened, demoralized remnants of the prison-guard Liberated would be no match for a full Federation combat team.

She pounded on the subspace communicator relay. *"Emissary's* . . . I mean, *Deep Space Nine* to Captain Taggart, *Deep Space Nine* to Captain Taggart of the *U.S.S. Harriman,* urgent communication!"

The reedy voice popped out of the air. "This is *Rear Admiral* Taggart of the *Harriman*. Whom am I addressing?"

"This is Major Kira. Admiral, I lowered the shields, and the dean and top officers of the alien invaders are casualties."

A long pause; too long. "Major Kira—if that *is* your name—I have no assurances that this is not a ruse to lure my ship within striking range and capture some more hostages. I'm afraid I will have to investigate the situation thoroughly before committing any more human resources to what is unarguably a deteriorating situation."

At that moment the turbolift ghosted silently downward. If her eyes hadn't been opened by then and looking the right direction, she would have missed its departure. Kira watched the shaft intently . . . who would come up?

Far below, she heard it coming. She was so intent on the shaft that when a meaty forefinger tapped her on the shoulder, she nearly jumped right out of her skin and danced around in her bones. She whirled to face a pale human face carrying a phaser rifle and wearing a Starfleet uniform. A voice spoke authoritatively behind her. "Major Kira of the Bajoran Defense Forces?"

She whirled back, dizzy enough to grab the communications console for support. There was a triplet of black-clad soldiers in the turbolift, holding their rifles at port-arms. "Major Kira," she whispered, hardly daring to breathe.

"Commander Vincent Fie, of the *Harriman*. Captain's apologies, but as he said, it was necessary to investigate further and confirm your identity. That investigation took a bit of doing, but I hereby confirm your identity and you'll be pleased to know this starbase has been secured."

Kai Winn improved dramatically in the infirmary, after the *Harriman* sent its surgeon to seal up her back. Kira's blow had been more precise than she had a right to demand, given the circumstances, and the major vowed to light incense and offer up thirty prayer-cycles to the Prophets in thanksgiving for Their timely guiding of her hand. The knife cut deeply into the Kai's shoulder, creating lots of realistic bleeding, but it missed all the innards and didn't even shatter the clavicle. Winn regained consciousness after the operation, and within a day was running the entire station again through the comlink, using her loyal fighting team as hands and eyes.

Kira waited to be summoned, either to be thanked (if the Kai understood why Kira had stabbed her) or informed in crystal terms that the major had made a deadly enemy. But the call never came. Kira fretted at the silence, but there was no one to ask about it except Garak . . . *and I'm not that desperate,* she vowed.

Garak returned to his cutting and stitching, refusing to take a hand in the wrenching cleanup. But the O'Briens pitched in, and Jake too, anxious at last to be doing something. By the time the *Defiant* came strolling back, *Emissary's Sanctuary* would be in fine condition for the farewell ceremonies for Captain (not Admiral) Benjamin Sisko and the rest of his

Starfleet crew. *Emissary's Sanctuary* would truly, wholly, be Bajoran at last.

So why don't I rejoice? Kira asked herself . . . but answer came there none, not even from the voice of the Prophets. *If even They're confused,* she thought miserably, *what hope do I have to make sense of these warring feelings?*

Major Kira slowly swept up broken glass from the Promenade floor, shunning the automated systems that would do such menial cleaning for her. She looked forward with alternating dread and eagerness to that final moment when they—when Bajor— would truly spin in its own orbit. *Maybe that's also what the Kai is waiting for,* thought Kira, swallowing a lump of anxiety. She felt like a little kid in school who's been promised a beating by the class sadist, watching the clock tick inexorably toward recess, when she would be *alone* with him and there'd be no teachers around to intervene.

But there was no *Defiant,* and no word. Kira, and even the Kai (or so she said through her proxies), began to wonder and worry. And whatever *had* happened to the Orb???

CHAPTER
17

CHIEF O'BRIEN still felt a wee tad green about the gills, despite (or due to) having digested his fair share of an extract of the native plant life. There was a horrible taste he couldn't get rid of crawling up and down his gizzard like the creatures were back to life, skittering from stomach to throat and down again, rattling around inside his gullet. O'Brien felt nauseated, but he fought the feeling: it was a far piece from the near-death experience of the cyanogen poisoning, though Bashir still didn't know whether there was any permanent damage. And the lurching of the diesel jalopy wasn't helping O'Brien's stomach either.

I got the worst of it, thought the chief. *I was the weak link. I nearly brought us down.* Even Quark fared better, though to be honest the Ferengi fared better than anyone except Odo, who didn't count.

"I finally figured out why you were so little affected," said Odo to his nemesis, eerily echoing O'Brien's own thoughts.

Quark was distracted, still staring at the ground receding behing them as if it were the Glory Road itself . . . which, considering the latinum content, it probably was to a Ferengi. Had Quark been paying attention, he never would have walked into the goo. "What? Why?"

He seemed to realize he'd blundered into a verbal trap and tried to grab the words back, but Odo was too quick. "Because you're already so corrupt to the core that the cyanogens had no effect. They tried and tried, but you're so poisonous, they simply gave it up."

"Oh, ho ho ho!" *He must be exhausted,* thought O'Brien, *or he'd at least have responded.*

The lorry jerked, crashing over a fallen tree stump, nearly flinging the chief from his perch atop the giant gearbox. One of the wheels caught on the stump and tore off; another wheel fell from inside somewhere and dropped into place, picking up the load on the other side of the tree.

The chief stared back in amazement at the lost wheel receding behind them, then at the new one, complete with flexible mechanical ankle, that had taken its place. The ignorant genius of the Natives terrified him. They were innocent of even the simplest engineering knowledge and busily reinventing the wheel—literally—at a pace of centuries per day. "Lord knows," muttered O'Brien, not intending to be overheard, "where they'll be same time next year."

"If we even recognize them," said Captain Sisko, staring fixedly into his box of Native toys, items of new tech that would expand the Federation technobase immeasurably . . . if O'Brien or some Earthbound engineer could figure out how they worked.

"Beg pardon, sir?" O'Brien felt his face heat up. He really had been talking to himself.

But Dax took up the conversational line. She sat on the hood itself, directly atop the engine, but didn't appear to be burning herself. "When we came here, we were worried that our technology might contaminate this culture, exposing them to devices they weren't prepared to handle. . . ."

The chief looked as Sisko, a question in his eyes. "And?" *Why don't the Native diesel engines get hot?* he wondered.

"I'm wondering if we should bring this box of gadgets home with us, or just leave them right here. I'd hate to contaminate our culture with technology we're not ready for."

"Julian?" Dax asked suddenly, looking back to the passenger compartment, "are you still with us?"

The doctor sat apart from the others, the only one to end up in an actual seat, next to the little girl Tivva-ma, who drove. (Since she was approximately the same age as Molly, O'Brien sweated rivers whenever he caught sight of her behind the navigation console.)

Bashir responded only with a grunt. He cradled his chin on joined fists and stared at the horizon. *He's probably got the plant-throat even worse than I,* thought O'Brien. After all, the chief had merely "eaten" plant extract, while Bashir was the one who

224

had actually manufactured it. He knew far better than the chief exactly what they had eaten.

The shaking, belching, noxious diesel truck, with its regenerating wheels, perfect heat-exchanger, and (seemingly) no steering wheel, remained perfectly on course, according to Dax and her tricorder. The captain asked something, but had to repeat himself as Chief O'Brien was holding his throat, wondering whether the terrible aftertaste would ever go away.

"Chief? Are we close enough yet to use the radio transmitter?"

"What? Oh, sorry, sir." They traveled through a forest of tall bluewoods that alternately blocked the sun and allowed it to shine full-force on the chief's modified com-badge, which he had opened in order to rewire the guts. He cupped his hand over it, squinting with aging eyes at the tiny, intricate circuits. He was looking for a carrier-wave response on the transceiver pack. It was just starting to glow tangerine orange. "Uh, looks like it's ready, Captain."

O'Brien carefully handed the disassembled com-badge to Sisko. "Don't, ah, let these two pieces get more than—there, keep them close. Just hold the relay shut and speak normally."

"Sisko to *Defiant*," said the captain with no preamble, dramatic speech, or magic gestures. He spoke as a man who expected a response, nothing less.

He got one. "Captain, you're alive!" shrieked the tinny, unrealistic-sounding voice. *Damn*, thought the perfectionist chief, *not enough bandwidth even to sound recognizable*. It could be anybody from Ensign

Wabak to a refuse-maintenance technician, but Sisko seemed satisfied.

"Whom am I speaking to?"

"En—Ens—Ensign Weymouth, sir," she said, sounding shaken even over the narrow-banded radio carrier.

"Yes, Ensign Weymouth, we all are alive," said the captain, "and we will be at the seashore near the ship in . . . Dax?"

The Trill choked down a Cardassian rice-ball and spat her estimate around it. "Two days, if we don't stop for sightseeing."

"In two days, Ensign Weymouth." Sisko grinned. "So slay the fatted calf. Prepare the ship for immediate launch to orbit once you've picked us up."

The chief heard a terrible rumbling. Reacting as an old soldier, he flattened himself on the gearbox faceup and drew his phaser. Two large dots appeared at five o'clock position, from behind O'Brien's left boot, from his perspective. He watched them nervously for some time before realizing what they were.

It was a flight of two Native *airships,* grinding their way across the sky with some sort of internal-combustion engine driving a series of screws at the back of each airship. The screws pushed the ships through the sky in a similar fashion to old Earth "propellers," except with a push instead of a pull.

"My God," shouted the chief as the airships buzzed the lorry column, much to the delighted whooping of the Natives. "My God, five weeks ago they couldn't work a bloody lever and had never heard of rope." He shook his head in two parts disbelief, three parts terror, as the airships flashed

226

past and disappeared over the eleven-o'clock horizon.

Captain Sisko held his breath as the *Defiant* burst off the ground, now carrying her full crew complement, and lusted for high orbit. The back of his neck itched, and he could almost feel the big guns of Sierra-Bravo 112-II shredding his ship like a hammer into a stack of potato chips.

The blow never came. *Maybe we got out before they spotted us. Maybe the defenses recognized that we were leaving and chose not to hinder us.*

But for whatever reason, the *Defiant* rose swiftly and unhindered; ship and crew were, at long last, heading finally, inexorably, home. Home, after a brief stop to disgorge prisoners.

But to what? We have no home. A wave of sadness washed over Benjamin Sisko. *Deep Space Nine,* newly renamed, by now surely spiffed up according to Kai Winn inspection standards, would be only a way-station for him and his team—his family of the past four years—a transit zone to await diaspora to their new commands. Major Kira—and presumably Quark and Odo, who were not under Federation discipline—would stay. Everyone else, everyone, would leave.

The circle is split
And becomes
A succession of lazy snakes leading
Everywhere astray
Of where my heart rang slowly
Like a bell

—An unknown Klingon, chronicling one of the riffs of the endless Klingon saga of conquest and exile.

What next? "Whither then, we cannot say."

"Could you please repeat that?" asked Worf, scowling back from the nearby weapons console.

"No," said Captain Sisko, gently closing the subject. The gaps were calling, and he must obey.

He leaned his head back, recalling their leave-taking from Sierra-Bravo 112-II. It warmed the heart considerably more than the abbreviated departure from what once had been *Deep Space Nine,* full of urgencies, recriminations, second thoughts, and the extraordinary condescension of Kai Winn, an awe-inspiring force unto herself.

This time, Asta-ha had struggled against crying, while tiny Tivva-ma had clutched Odo in a death-grip around his knees, ordering him not to depart— and following that with a frighteningly adult list of more than a dozen reasons, including that he was needed to "help develop and implement my newest judicial compact." Still, chillingly developed intelligence did not make her any less a little girl, and she offered to allow Chief O'Brien to take her invisible friend Datha-ma back to be a playmate for "Molly-ma." That brought the chief to.

What would happen to them? Was Bashir right, that a mere eleven million Natives were not viable without their new tech? Or was Dax correct, that the Natives—especially Colonel-Mayor Asta-ha and her Vanimastavvi—were more than capable?

Another dilemma: should the Federation return or leave the Natives alone to solve their own problems? *And what sort of homecoming should we expect?* pondered the captain. The command chair, which should have fitted Sisko like a tight uniform, felt loose, broken, and creaky. "Chief O'Brien," he said, "I think this seat needs maintenance."

Sisko rose, took a last, last look at the star system, already nothing more than a faint dot, that was Sierra-Bravo and her dark sister Stirnis. It was receding. No, it was gone: the tiny speck of flame was an after-image in the rear viewer or perhaps his own retina. There would be no more Natives for Benjamin Sisko, not again.

"They'll probably assign us together, Old Man," he said, not looking at Dax.

"Probably. We work well together, and you have pull."

Captain Sisko looked down at his command console, which O'Brien was already tearing apart per instructions. When he looked up again, Dax was just Dax, his Old Man. Nothing more. It was always the way.

"I suspect the Kai will be more than happy to see us, Dax," he said.

"So pleased," said she, "that she'll probably throw us a farewell banquet . . . in the launch bay, all the better not to delay our final departure."

Somewhere behind Sisko, Odo gave his characteristic snort, and Worf was characteristically silent.

Quark scurried past carrying a bucket and a mop.

After a private talk with the captain, Odo had relented and agreed not to formally charge the Ferengi with the dozen or so counts the constable had accumulated in his ledger—*if* Quark agreed to scrub the entire *Defiant* from stem to stern on the way back. Sisko shut his ears to the dreadful oaths and curses erupting from the Ferengi as he went about his cheerless task: the interplay between cop and crook was a force of nature, and Sisko made a habit of never interfering with the weather.

He glanced at the woman he had spoken to on the radio, Ensign Weymouth. "Ensign, set a course for . . . ah, what's it called again?"

"The station?" she asked, sounding suddenly unsure herself of the new name. *Or maybe she's just afraid to show up the captain in front of the bridge crew.*

"Yes, that thing. *Emissary's Sanctuary,* that's it. Full steam ahead."

The summons finally came, calling Major Kira before the Kai. She had dreaded the audience, but resented its delay. When she finally received the order to come to Ops immediately, Kira found she had flits in her stomach as bad as the first time she met the new Federation commander of *Deep Space Nine,* of *Terok Nor. If he had been the Emissary too, back then,* she thought, *I probably would have run back to Bajor rather than face him!*

Swallowing, Kira left the panel of the bombardment shelter dangling. There were maintenance techs better equipped than she to repair the circuitry, restoring the ability of occupants to open the door without requiring an electronic key from the outside. She brushed herself off, tugged her uniform vaguely straight, rejected the momentary thought of rushing back to her quarters to freshen up, and headed instead directly for the nearest turbolift.

When she rose into Ops, the Kai's "cell group" was running the place, as usual, and Winn herself was up in her ready-room. *She sure has mastered the art of delegating authority,* thought the major uncharitably.

Tugging at her collar as she climbed the ladderway and tonguing her new tooth, Kira offered a brief prayer and apology to the Prophets for the thought. She stepped forward to ring the twitter, but the unlocked door opened instead, leaving Kira with raised hand.

"Do stop gaping, child, and sit down." Kai Winn barely glanced up at her until she did as instructed. Then Winn put away the report she had been reading, carefully turned off her desk viewer, and settled her hands together, smiling in her special way.

"I received subspace communications from the Emissary. He is on his way back."

Kira's voice caught momentarily in her throat. Too many emotions. She took a deep breath. "Did he find any Cardassians or Jem'Hadar?"

"Cardassians and Drek'la, but no Dominion forces. Not that he mentioned. It was a very terse message, child."

"Any—casualties?"

"None. He was quite emphatic about that, insisting that I tell you personally." The Kai sounded peeved at being ordered to do anything by anybody, even the Emissary to the Prophets. *She probably wouldn't like the Prophets themselves manifesting and ordering her out for tea things.*

"Yes, my Kai. Thank you. Anything else?"

"We have retrieved the Orb safely."

Kira hesitated. "May I be permitted to ask where you hid it?"

Winn smiled, always pleased to be able to demonstrate her astuteness. "Why child, when the aliens invaded, I simply put the Orb into the garbage shoot and ejected it into space. I concluded the airlessness wouldn't hurt it, and it would be easy enough to retrieve it when the invaders left . . . *all* of them," she added—signifying the recently departed Starfleet admiral.

Kira was truly impressed. "I never would have thought of that! You are rightly Kai. Um, anything else? Involving *me?*"

"Yes. Major, what is your assessment of the repairs? Are they progressing rapidly enough? I'm disturbed by how much of the station continues to show evidence of the recent unpleasantness."

Kira paused a long time before speaking. "Kai, we really have to talk about it."

"Yes, I think it's high time we talk about the progress of repairs."

"Not that. We have to talk about what I—"

"Repairs are vital if we are to greet the Emissary as he properly deserves, child. How about young Jake Sisko? Is he going to be, well, presentable?"

"Presentable?" Kira again tried to interrupt the runaway dreadnought of the Kai's discourse, but she was thwarted once more.

"I seem to recall a recent unpleasantness with him and a Dabo girl. I would be mortified on behalf of all Bajor, if the Emissary were to return and find his only son and heir in the arms of a young lady of loose character several years his senior."

Kira stared, frustrated and astonished. "You're not going to talk about it. You're not going to talk about what happened during our own little Resistance, are you?"

Winn shrugged, dismissing a trivial subject. "We resisted, child. Now please give me a full report on the progress of restoration."

Kira waited a long moment, then smiled coldly herself and gave a spontaneous but thorough analysis of the state of repairs. Just as she finished, the com-link chirped.

"Kai," said the voice of one of her cell members, "the Cardassian tailor wishes to see you."

"Send him right up," said the Kai blissfully. She leaned forward to whisper to Kira. "I truly can't stand the plotter, but what can I do? I am governor to all who live on this station . . . for however long they continue to do so."

The door slid open and Garak entered, looking like the dog who swallowed the breakfast, if that is the expression. "Good morning, ladies. I didn't expect to find *you* here, Major Kira."

Kira stiffened. She knew what he was implying by the raised brow, the slight tilt to his head, the curled lip. But there was nothing overtly wrong with what he had said, so she sat quietly and made no response. *Some of the Kai's diplomacy must be rubbing off on me,* she thought glumly.

"Yes, Mr. Garak, may I be of assistance?"

"Oh no, Governor, it is I who shall be your servant in this! I'm playing message carrier today, bringing you information from some of my close friends back on Bajor." Kira could not help making a noise, but neither conversant paid her any mind.

"A message from Bajor? Odd," said the Kai, smiling as she had when speaking to the late dean, "I have heard nothing."

"Ah, then it's a good thing I have." Garak restarted his interrupted progress to her desk and laid a data clip in front of her. "This is an intercepted communication between your friend and mine, Minister Shakaar—your friend too, Major!—and two of his erstwhile cellmates. Oh, I do beg your pardon. Of course, I meant cell members."

Kai Winn glanced down at the clip but made no move to pick it up. "Was this a privileged communication? I would have thought our governmental encryption methods were hard enough to prevent a mere tailor from breaking them."

"I? I am merely the passive receptacle. I haven't even read the communication. But I'm sure it's important."

"Oh?" said Kira. "How would you know that?"

"I suspect it has to do with the unannounced vote tomorrow in the Bajoran Council."

A *bickett* chirping would have echoed in the totally silent ready room. Both Bajorans waited expectantly.

"My word," said Garak, pretending surprise, "you haven't even heard?"

"I have heard about no vote in the Council chambers tomorrow."

The Cardassian spymaster tsk-tsked, shaking his head. "I understand it has to do with the future of Bajor. Specifically, who is to govern the planet itself."

"Why," said Winn dangerously, "we have all agreed that the Kai—in consultation with the minsters, of course—should set the course for—"

"Now that the Kai is too busy as acting governor of *Terok Nor* to be bothered by the trivialities of day-to-day governance of Bajor itself."

Kira rose. From Kai Winn's expression, it was evident that the meeting was over . . . and undoubtedly, that the Kai would very quickly be calling for her belongings to be shoveled into a runabout as she shrieked away toward the planet to rally her somnambulant troops and partisans, polywogs and hangers-on, groupies and agitators to start a belated and possibly futile campaign against the vote. "I have finished my report, Kai Winn," said the major. "May I leave?"

Winn said nothing, staring at the data clip as if it were a dead lizard on her desk. "I should be going as well," said Garak; "I have cloth to cut, coats to sew, and such. Good day, Governor." He bowed and followed on Kira's heels out the door and down the ladderway, his own boots almost kicking the major in her forehead as they raced each other (in a dignified way) to the turbolift.

As they dropped, Kira turned to the Cardassian.

"Now that's an interesting turn. You didn't like it much, her being here, did you?"

Garak raised his brows yet again. "Why, Major. Whatever are you accusing me of? Do you think a humble Cardassian would have the ear of certain dissident elements on Bajor? Could a tailor move the mighty Shakar to attempt a coup d'etat? In any event, I suspect Kai Winn will be too busy dealing with the political wildfires on Bajor to worry overmuch about the station reverting into Federation hands, as many in the Federation Council have wanted all along."

Kira said nothing. But she smiled and didn't even care that Garak could see her appreciation. *And why're you so happy?* she accused herself. *Bajor has been humiliated. When will Bajor's finally be Bajor's?*

But she shrugged off the patriotic voice. Bajor had enough problems *being* Bajor without taking on the role of Master of *Terok Nor* as well, with all the emotional and psychological baggage it brought. All in all, she decided it was probably best that the station remain *Deep Space Nine,* with Benjamin Sisko, Emissary to the Prophets, in charge, rather than Kai Winn.

For now, she added. *At least for now. But with the Kai's damned spy-eyes ripped out,* she promised herself.

"Computer," she said abruptly, as the doors opened on the Promenade and Garak exited. "Locate Jake Sisko."

"Jake Sisko is in Quark's, third level."

Kira stepped out of the turbolift, headed toward

Quark's. She figured Jake (and whoever he might be with) would appreciate the heads-up that his old man was on the way back.

Three Federation years after first contact was initiated with the natives of Sierra-Bravo 112-II ("the Natives," as the original contact team called them), the *U.S.S. Malloc* dropped out of warp at the proper coordinates. It was a small ship, fast and lightly armed, useful for scouting, diplomatic missions, and setting up a contact readvisory team on "contaminated" worlds.

"Ensign," said Captain Mirok, a Vulcan admiral in the ambassadorial corps, "please initiate a geo-synchronous orbit outside the reported range of the planetary defense systems. We will send down a cloaked shuttle to contact the Natives." Mirok's dignity was somewhat offended by the flippant name, which had unfortunately stuck. The first order of business would be to construct a better way to refer to the natives.

"Sir?" asked Ensign Weymouth, newly transferred to his command. He already regretted her hesitation and found her lapses of judgment troubling.

"Put the ship into a high orbit, Ensign. Is there a problem?"

"There's. . . ." She faded out, looking blank. "There's nothing to orbit *around*, sir."

"Are these the correct coordinates, Lieutenant?"

Lieutenant Pas, another Vulcan—for obvious reasons, the ship had a heavy Vulcan contingent—rechecked the navigation system. "Yes, sir. We are at the correct coordinates, and the star on the forward viewer is, in fact, Sierra-Bravo 112. Stirnis is in its correct place. But the ensign is correct: there is no second planet in the recorded orbit."

Mirok raised an eyebrow. "Debris?"

"None," said Pas. "Neither is there any echo of weaponry that could have destroyed the planet." The lieutenant rose from his science-console scope. "The planet is missing, and there is no explanation that I can think of. It is simply gone."

Mirok raised the other eyebrow, then stood. "Initiate a search pattern. If we cannot find the planet or any evidence in three days, we must return to the Federation and make our report."

"I suspect the diplomatic corps and the Council will not be pleased at the report," said Pas.

"I suspect your prediction is correct," said the captain. "Nevertheless, there is no other logical course of action. Proceed."

Captain Mirok stepped around the turbolift to return to his ready-room, already sketching in his orderly mind the diplomatic gymnastics he would have to perform to soothe the emotional humans who still ran the Federation Council as if by hereditary right.

But he couldn't help wondering: what in the name of Surak *had* happened to an entire planet full of intellectually supercharged Natives? *They could not have taken their planet and simply left. Or could they?*

Look for STAR TREK Fiction from Pocket Books

Star Trek®: The Original Series

Star Trek: The Motion Picture • Gene Roddenberry
Star Trek II: The Wrath of Khan • Vonda N. McIntyre
Star Trek III: The Search for Spock • Vonda N. McIntyre
Star Trek IV: The Voyage Home • Vonda N. McIntyre
Star Trek V: The Final Frontier • J. M. Dillard
Star Trek VI: The Undiscovered Country • J. M. Dillard
Star Trek VII: Generations • J. M. Dillard
Star Trek VIII: First Contact • J. M. Dillard
Star Trek IX: Insurrection • J. M. Dillard
Enterprise: The First Adventure • Vonda N. McIntyre
Final Frontier • Diane Carey
Strangers from the Sky • Margaret Wander Bonanno
Spock's World • Diane Duane
The Lost Years • J. M. Dillard
Probe • Margaret Wander Bonanno
Prime Directive • Judith and Garfield Reeves-Stevens
Best Destiny • Diane Carey
Shadows on the Sun • Michael Jan Friedman
Sarek • A. C. Crispin
Federation • Judith and Garfield Reeves-Stevens
The Ashes of Eden • William Shatner & Judith and Garfield
  Reeves-Stevens
The Return • William Shatner & Judith and Garfield Reeves-
  Stevens
Star Trek: Starfleet Academy • Diane Carey
Vulcan's Forge • Josepha Sherman and Susan Shwartz
Avenger • William Shatner & Judith and Garfield Reeves-Stevens
Star Trek: Odyssey • William Shatner & Judith and Garfield
  Reeves-Stevens

#1 *Star Trek: The Motion Picture* • Gene Roddenberry
#2 *The Entropy Effect* • Vonda N. McIntyre
#3 *The Klingon Gambit* • Robert E. Vardeman
#4 *The Covenant of the Crown* • Howard Weinstein
#5 *The Prometheus Design* • Sondra Marshak & Myrna
    Culbreath
#6 *The Abode of Life* • Lee Correy
#7 *Star Trek II: The Wrath of Khan* • Vonda N. McIntyre

Star Trek: The Next Generation®

Star Trek: Deep Space Nine®

The Search • Diane Carey
Warped • K. W. Jeter
The Way of the Warrior • Diane Carey
Star Trek: Klingon • Dean W. Smith & Kristine K. Rusch
Trials and Tribble-ations • Diane Carey
Far Beyond the Stars • Steve Barnes
The 34th Rule • Armin Shimerman & David George

#1 *Emissary* • J. M. Dillard
#2 *The Siege* • Peter David
#3 *Bloodletter* • K. W. Jeter
#4 *The Big Game* • Sandy Schofield
#5 *Fallen Heroes* • Dafydd ab Hugh
#6 *Betrayal* • Lois Tilton
#7 *Warchild* • Esther Friesner
#8 *Antimatter* • John Vornholt
#9 *Proud Helios* • Melissa Scott
#10 *Valhalla* • Nathan Archer
#11 *Devil in the Sky* • Greg Cox & John Greggory Betancourt
#12 *The Laertian Gamble* • Robert Sheckley
#13 *Station Rage* • Diane Carey
#14 *The Long Night* • Dean W. Smith & Kristine K. Rusch
#15 *Objective: Bajor* • John Peel
#16 *Invasion #3: Time's Enemy* • L. A. Graf
#17 *The Heart of the Warrior* • John Greggory Betancourt
#18 *Saratoga* • Michael Jan Friedman
#19 *The Tempest* • Susan Wright
#20 *Wrath of the Prophets* • P. David, M. J. Friedman,
    R. Greenberger
#21 *Trial by Error* • Mark Garland
#22 *Vengeance* • Dafydd ab Hugh
#23 *The Conquered: Rebels, Book One* • Dafydd ab Hugh
#24 *The Courageous: Rebels, Book Two* • Dafydd ab Hugh
#25 *The Liberated: Rebels, Book Three* • Dafydd ab Hugh

Star Trek®: Voyager™

Flashback • Diane Carey
The Black Shore • Greg Cox
Mosaic • Jeri Taylor

#1 *Caretaker* • L. A. Graf
#2 *The Escape* • Dean W. Smith & Kristine K. Rusch
#3 *Ragnarok* • Nathan Archer
#4 *Violations* • Susan Wright
#5 *Incident at Arbuk* • John Greggory Betancourt
#6 *The Murdered Sun* • Christie Golden
#7 *Ghost of a Chance* • Mark A. Garland & Charles G. McGraw
#8 *Cybersong* • S. N. Lewitt
#9 *Invasion #4: The Final Fury* • Dafydd ab Hugh
#10 *Bless the Beasts* • Karen Haber
#11 *The Garden* • Melissa Scott
#12 *Chrysalis* • David Niall Wilson
#13 *The Black Shore* • Greg Cox
#14 *Marooned* • Christie Golden
#15 *Echoes* • Dean W. Smith & Kristine K. Rusch
#16 *Seven of Nine* • Christie Golden

Star Trek®: New Frontier

#1 *House of Cards* • Peter David
#2 *Into the Void* • Peter David
#3 *The Two-Front War* • Peter David
#4 *End Game* • Peter David
#5 *Martyr* • Peter David
#6 *Fire on High* • Peter David

Star Trek®: Day of Honor

Book One: *Ancient Blood* • Diane Carey
Book Two: *Armageddon Sky* • L. A. Graf
Book Three: *Her Klingon Soul* • Michael Jan Friedman
Book Four: *Treaty's Law* • Dean W. Smith & Kristine K. Rusch

Star Trek®: The Captain's Table

Book One: *War Dragons* • L. A. Graf
Book Two: *Dujonian's Hoard* • Michael Jan Friedman
Book Three: *The Mist* • Dean W. Smith & Kristine K. Rusch
Book Four: *Fire Ship* • Diane Carey
Book Five: *Once Burned* • Peter David
Book Six: *Where Sea Meets Sky* • Jerry Oltion

Star Trek®: The Dominion War

Book 1: *Behind Enemy Lines* • John Vornholt
Book 2: *Call to Arms . . .* • Diane Carey
Book 3: *Tunnel Through the Stars* • John Vornholt
Book 4: *. . . Sacrifice of Angels* • Diane Carey

STAR TREK
DEEP SPACE NINE™

24" X 36" CUT AWAY POSTER,
7 COLORS WITH 2 METALLIC INKS & A GLOSS AND MATTE VARNISH, PRINTED ON ACID FREE ARCHIVAL QUALITY
65# COVER WEIGHT STOCK INCLUDES OVER 90 TECHNICAL CALLOUTS, AND HISTORY OF THE SPACE STATION.
U.S.S. DEFIANT EXTERIOR, HEAD SHOTS OF MAIN CHARACTERS, INCREDIBLE GRAPHIC OF WORMHOLE.

STAR TREK™
U.S.S. ENTERPRISE™ NCC-1701

24" X 36" CUT AWAY POSTER,
6 COLORS WITH A SPECIAL METALLIC INK & A GLOSS AND MATTE VARNISH, PRINTED ON ACID FREE ARCHIVAL
QUALITY 100# TEXT WEIGHT STOCK INCLUDES OVER 100 TECHNICAL CALLOUTS,
HISTORY OF THE ENTERPRISE CAPTAINS & THE HISTORY OF THE ENTERPRISE SHIPS.

ALSO AVAILABLE:
LIMITED EDITION SIGNED AND NUMBERED BY ARTISTS.
LITHOGRAPHIC PRINTS ON 80# COVER STOCK (DS9 ON 100 # STOCK) WITH OFFICIAL LICENSED CERTIFICATE OF
AUTHENTICITY. QT. AVAILABLE 2,500

Deep Space Nine Poster
Poster Qt. ___ @ $19.95 each _____
Limited Edition Poster
Poster Qt. ___ @ $40.00 each _____
U.S.S. Enterprise NCC-1701-E Poster
Poster Qt. ___ @ $19.95 each _____
Limited Edition Poster
Poster Qt. ___ @ $40.00 each _____
U.S.S. Enterprise NCC-1701 Poster
Poster Qt. ___ @ $14.95 each _____
Limited Edition Poster
Poster Qt. ___ @ $30.00 each _____
$4 Shipping U.S. Each _____
$10 Shipping Foreign Each _____
Michigan Residents Add 6% Tax _____
TOTAL _____

METHOD OF PAYMENT (U.S. FUNDS ONLY)
❏ Check ❏ Money Order ❏ MasterCard ❏ Visa
Account #

_ _ _ _ - _ _ _ _ - _ _ _ _ - _ _ _ _

Card Expiration Date ___ /___(Mo./Yr.)

Your Day Time Phone (___) - _____

_____
Your Signature

SHIP TO ADDRESS:
NAME:_____
ADDRESS:_____
CITY:_____ STATE:_____
POSTAL CODE:_____ COUNTRY:_____

Mail, Phone, or Fax Orders to:
SciPubTech • 15318 Mack Avenue • Grosse Pointe Park • Michigan 48230
Phone 313.884.6882 Fax 313.885.7426 Web Site http://www.scipubtech.com

ST5196